"I've wanted to ki *you, Tess. I've even dreamed about it, but I never meant to hurt you," Dan said.*

Her breath caught and her eyes fixed on the freckle at the corner of his mouth. "You wanted?"

He gave a rueful smile. "It doesn't matter."

Her knees were going weak, and she was mesmerized by the closeness of him. "Why not?" she whispered.

"I haven't felt much like a man since I left the hospital," he said slowly.

"Oh, good grief!" Tess grabbed the back of his head, pulled his face to hers, and planted a kiss on Dan Friday that would have unraveled his socks, if he'd been wearing any. He groaned as his arms came around her, gathering her body against his. His mouth moved over hers like that of a starving man at a feast, tasting, devouring, savoring.

Heat flashed between them like spontaneous combustion. Tess had never felt anything so potent, so overwhelming in her life. Gasping for breath, she pulled back and looked into his passion-darkened eyes. "Lord, Friday, you feel like a man to me. . . ."

WHAT ARE *LOVESWEPT* ROMANCES?

They are stories of true romance and touching emotion. We believe those two very important ingredients are constants in our highly sensual and very believable stories in the *LOVESWEPT* line. Our goal is to give you, the reader, stories of consistently high quality that may sometimes make you laugh, sometimes make you cry, but are always fresh and creative and contain many delightful surprises within their pages.

Most romance fans read an enormous number of books. Those they truly love, they keep. Others may be traded with friends and soon forgotten. We hope that each *LOVESWEPT* romance will be a treasure—a "keeper." We will always try to publish

LOVE STORIES YOU'LL NEVER FORGET
BY AUTHORS YOU'LL ALWAYS REMEMBER

The Editors

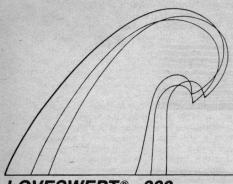

LOVESWEPT® • 380

Jan Hudson
Always Friday

BANTAM BOOKS
NEW YORK • TORONTO • LONDON • SYDNEY • AUCKLAND

ALWAYS FRIDAY

A Bantam Book / February 1990

*LOVESWEPT® and the wave device are registered
trademarks of Bantam Books, a division of
Bantam Doubleday Dell Publishing Group, Inc.
Registered in U.S. Patent
and Trademark Office and elsewhere.*

*If you would be interested in receiving protective vinyl
covers for your Loveswept books, please write to this address
for information:*

> *Loveswept
> Bantam Books
> P.O. Box 985
> Hicksville, NY 11802*

ISBN 0-553-44011-X

Published simultaneously in the United States and Canada

*Bantam Books are published by Bantam Books, a division
of Bantam Doubleday Dell Publishing Group, Inc. Its trademark, consisting of the words "Bantam Books" and the
portrayal of a rooster, is Registered in U.S. Patent and
Trademark Office and in other countries. Marca Registrada.
Bantam Books, 666 Fifth Avenue, New York, New York 10103.*

PRINTED IN THE UNITED STATES OF AMERICA

O   0 9 8 7 6 5 4 3 2 1

For Mother, with love,
and for all the special Lindas in my life

One

"Ain't nobody here but me, and I'm just fixing the furnace. Think Hook drove the ladies over somewhere in Louisiana to see that flower garden. Everybody says it's right pretty this time of year with the tulips and such. I believe they're all gone for the weekend, except Tess."

Damn! The muscles in Daniel Friday's jaw twitched as he clenched his teeth, and the deep lines between his eyebrows became furrows. Why in the hell couldn't Gram stay put for one day? Now of all times, when he was swamped with work, he couldn't believe he'd flown to Galveston for nothing. His sister Kathy had convinced him that their grandmother had moved in with a bunch of strange people who might very well be con artists of some kind, and she had insisted that he come check out the situation.

"Who's Tess?"

"Tess Cameron, Miss Olivia's niece. No," the stoop-shouldered man in blue coveralls said as he rubbed his chin, "I guess she'd be Miss Olivia's great-niece.

Her mama was the niece. Miss Octavia's daughter. Miss Octavia and Miss Olivia was—"

"Yes, yes. May I speak to—"

"—twin sisters, you know," the repairman drawled on, ignoring the brusque interruption. "Spittin' image of one another, but Miss Octavia's been gone about eight or ten years and her daughter closer to thirty. Anna, I recollect her name was." He rubbed his chin again. "Or was it Amelia? No, I believe it was Anna."

Daniel Friday was a man who valued his time. Tall and impeccably dressed, he was also one whose presence commanded respect, and he demanded the same competence and efficiency from others that he did from himself. He was accustomed to controlling every situation, and his irritation grew as he was forced to listen to the old geezer's meandering drone. Not even Daniel's sternest "let's cut the crap and get on with business" look, a look guaranteed to sober every one of his employees immediately, could faze the fellow.

Daniel stood on the porch of the old mansion on Galveston's main thoroughfare, shifting his weight from one foot to the other. Even the magnificent three-storied redbrick house, which at first glance he judged to be well over a hundred years old, captured only his subliminal awareness. All he wanted was to find his grandmother, get her settled back where she belonged, and return to Pittsburgh first thing tomorrow. Maybe the niece could help him find Gram.

"May I speak to Tess?" Daniel asked when the man paused for a breath.

"She ain't here. Ain't nobody here but me."

Daniel waited for a long-winded explanation, but

this time, when one was needed, none was forth-coming. Dragging his fingers impatiently through his thick, tawny hair, he asked very deliberately, "Where can I find her?"

"I'm not right sure, but you could try the pier down at Twenty-Seventh and Seawall. She goes down there most mornings about this time. Says the fid-dler crabs don't complain about her music as much as the neighbors do. Yep, I'd try there first if I was you."

Fighting to control his growing frustration, Dan-iel secured directions from the repairman, stalked to his rental car, and headed toward the Gulf. The morning fog was so dense that he had to creep along and squint at the street signs. Mumbling about his rotten luck, he finally found the spot he was looking for, parked, and slammed the door as he got out.

A pain gnawed at his stomach. Heartburn again, he thought. Too much coffee and too little sleep. It seemed that there was never enough time these days, never enough of him to spread around. His twelve- and fourteen-hour days had been stretching into sixteen and eighteen. There were always labor prob-lems, equipment malfunctions, material delays, and the never-ending mounds of paperwork. Right now he needed to be in his office in Pittsburgh, not chasing after Gram and a gang of loonies on a foggy sandbar along the Texas coast.

A fine mist spotted his navy wool blazer as he crossed the boulevard, deserted as far as he could tell except for a lone jogger slapping the wet asphalt and a small black dog running beside him. Scents of fish and ocean and rotting wood hung heavy in the humid air. Though he couldn't see through the fog that hovered over both the island and the water, he could hear the cries of sea gulls overhead, mixed with the gentle lap of waves on the shore. The occasional blare of fog horns, some distant, some closer, echoed over the water as he descended the seawall steps.

He walked carefully onto the rock groin pier, following the sound of a strange whining he couldn't identify. It sounded almost like the skirl of a bagpipe coming from the misty fog. He had no idea how long the pier was, and he was hesitant to go much farther.

He called out. "Tess Cameron!" He listened for an answer, but all he heard was the haunting whine from the fog, the sea gulls, and water washing against the rocks.

Cautious of the slippery surface of the jetty under his leather-soled shoes, he advanced slowly and hoped to hell he didn't step off into the Gulf of Mexico. If he hadn't loved his grandmother so much, right about then he would have seriously considered throttling her. He muttered a few choice oaths and trekked on.

He had gone about thirty feet out when he saw her.

The tall, slender figure playing the bagpipe was no dour Scot from the highlands. Instead of kilts and tartan, she wore orange overalls and a fuchsia shirt, and a floppy yellow rain hat pulled low over her ears. She was playing the bagpipe, playing with total abandon. And obviously relishing every minute of it.

The scene and the sounds and the piper were so totally incongruous that, in spite of his agitation he couldn't help but smile. Her whole body was animated as she played. Her head bobbed as her cheeks puffed and blew, her bottom did an exaggerated twitch, and her knees pumped up and down as her fingers moved along the chanter.

He wanted to laugh out loud. God, how long had it been since he had enjoyed anything as much as she was enjoying those bagpipes? For a moment, Gram and the pile of work on his desk were forgotten as he stuck his hands in his pockets, ambled a little closer, and stood watching her. The fog began to dissipate as the sun rose higher in the sky and heated the air with its warm rays. It almost seemed as if she were cranking up the sun and banishing the mist.

After several minutes she must have sensed his presence, for the mouthpiece dropped from her mouth and the melody died with a discordant whine as she turned toward him. At first she looked startled, then her face lit with a smile wide enough to burn off the morning fog. That smile slammed into his gut like a left jab.

"Good morning," she said. "I was afraid you were a fisherman who'd come to grouse at me about scaring off the fish."

Even her voice intrigued him. It was deep, husky, with a little catch that made him think of the hoarseness of someone who'd just awakened or was recovering from laryngitis.

"And what makes you think I'm not?" He moved closer, noticing as he neared how tall she was. He was six-foot-two and she was no more than four or five inches shorter.

Her eyes crinkled and her dimpled chin lifted as she laughed. "The fishermen around here don't wear silk ties." Her eyebrows, dark and slightly unruly, rose as she looked down. "Or Ferragamo loafers. If you're going to walk on the jetties, you'd be wise to get some rubber soles. You're gonna bust your butt in those."

"I don't have any other shoes with me," he said, smiling and looking into her open, animated face.

"Then go barefoot. It's safer, believe me."

Her eyes were as intriguing as her voice. They were a dancing kaleidoscope of blue, green, gold, and brown, and her dark lashes were thick and curly. A faint sprinkle of freckles across her nose told him she wore no makeup. But she needed none. Her cheeks were naturally blushed; her mouth was wide and her lips, pressed together in what he suspected was a perennial expression of amusement, were full and eminently kissable.

In fact, Daniel could think of nothing he'd like more at this very moment than to see if they tasted like strawberries.

A funny little flush rippled over Tess Cameron as she stared up at the man who stood only inches away from her. For a moment she had had the oddest feeling that he, a perfect stranger, was going to kiss her. It should have frightened her—for all she knew he could be some kind of pervert who stalked unsuspecting women—but it didn't.

She knew intuitively that she could trust him. Tess could tell a lot about people from their eyes. His were nice, a soft grayish blue that sparkled with his smile, and bespoke a man who was sincere and caring. Someone of substance.

He had a strong face with a high-bridged nose and ruggedly sculpted cheekbones and jaw. He exuded an almost palpable aura of quiet strength and determination. And he was tall enough for her to look up to. He was attractive. Definitely attractive.

No, she wasn't frightened of him, Tess thought as she looked into the gaze that sent another ripple darting through her awareness. What made her nervous was that she had the strongest urge to lift her face to encourage his kiss or to run her fingers through the thick mane of hair on his head that almost begged to be ruffled. This was crazy. Absolutely crazy. Totally alien to her previous experience. What was going on?

She tried to look away, but it was impossible. In the depths of those eyes that held hers with such a riveting intensity, she detected a hint of lingering sadness, or something akin to sadness, that grabbed at her heart and made her want to comfort him.

Ah, that was it. Something in her nature could home in on troubled people like a radar device. Her instinct to mother the world. Relieved once she could label her reaction, Tess took a step back. She couldn't explain the wobble in her knees, so she ignored it and glanced at the big wristwatch on her arm. "Oops, I'd better get going."

He seemed reluctant to let her go. "I was hoping you'd play some more. You're quite good."

She laughed again. "I wish you'd tell Angus that. He says I wiggle too much to ever be a proper piper."

"Angus?"

"Angus McFarland, my teacher. He plays with the Houston Symphony. I drive up a couple of times a month for lessons."

"He plays the bagpipe with the symphony?"

Eyes shining with amusement, she said, "No, he plays the flute. But he's wonderful on the bagpipe." She glanced at her watch again. "Listen, it's been great talking to you, but I've really got to go." She fluttered her fingers at him and took off up the pier with the bagpipe tucked under one arm. "Be careful with those shoes," she called over her shoulder.

Grinning in spite of himself, Daniel stood and

watched her long-legged stride as she disappeared into a lingering patch of fog. Was she for real? Then he started. "Hey, wait," he shouted. His shoes slipped as he hurried to catch up to her.

"Whoa there." As she reached out to steady him, she slipped herself. When they regained their footing, they found that both of his arms were around her, one of her arms around him, and the bagpipe crushed between them. Slowly she raised her gaze to his, and once more her knees started doing peculiar things. As she stood penned within the power and warmth of his arms, looking up at the marvelous planes of his face, her heartbeat seemed to develop an extra pitty-pat. And it was so loud she was sure he could hear it.

She managed to smile. "You almost landed on your keester."

"Thanks. I thought I was a goner for sure."

He laughed, showing beautiful, even teeth, and her knees grew even more wobbly. Why had she ever thought the reaction he aroused in her was maternal? Those were sexual signals she'd been receiving. Loud and clear.

She had to leave before she did or said something stupid like, Want to come to my place and see my etchings? He was, after all, a total stranger. Tess knew most of the people in town, and if he'd been one of them, she would have noticed *him*. He was probably a weekend tourist—though it wasn't yet tourist season—who would be gone tomorrow. He was probably married, anyway. It was beginning to seem as if all the good ones in her age group were either married or gay.

She tried to make her feet move, but they just didn't seem to want to obey.

His eyes scanned her face and he said softly, "I think you're the woman I'm looking for."

Her eyes widened. "I am?" Her voice was barely a whisper.

He nodded and was lowering his face to hers when he caught himself and stiffened. He seemed to shift gears as he dropped his arms and cleared his throat. "Are you Tess Cameron?"

Her eyebrows lifted. "Yes—" Her answer was tentative. She narrowed her eyes. "How did you know?"

"I was looking for my grandmother, and the man repairing the furnace said I might find you here."

Tess pursed her lips in amusement. "Do I look like your grandmother?"

He laughed and shook his head. "Hardly. My grandmother is only about so high." He held his hand level with Tess's shoulder. "And her name is Martha Craven. She's supposed to be living at Heritage House, but I understand she moved out."

"Ohhh, I see. You're Aunt Martha's grandson." Tess knew all about Martha Craven's grandsons, and neither of them was married. Or gay. "We love having her with us. She's a sweetheart. You must be either Danny or Teddy." She cocked her head. "I'd guess Danny."

He winced. "*Daniel* Friday. Or Dan. I haven't been called 'Danny' by anyone but my grandmother since I was ten years old."

"Dan Friday it is." She smiled and offered her hand. She noticed his hand was warm as he took hers. A good hand. Strong, like the rest of him, but with long fingers more suited to an artist than to a businessman. "How wonderful to have a name like Friday. It's always been my favorite day of the week. I used to spend most of my time wishing for Friday."

"And now?"

She laughed. "Now it's always Friday."

He smiled and his eyes shone with genuine pleasure as his gaze met hers. "Must be nice."

"It is. I'm sorry your grandmother isn't here. Hook drove her and Aunt Olivia over to Hodges Gardens. I'm sure she wouldn't have gone if she'd known you were coming."

"It was a spur-of-the-moment decision. When are they expected back?" Twin lines deepened between his eyebrows. "We have some important family business to discuss, but I need to return to Pittsburgh as soon as possible."

When he mentioned Pittsburgh, his whole manner changed. His warm smile had faded into a sort of a supercilious semi-scowl that reminded her of a preacher who'd suddenly discovered he was enjoying himself at a peep show. And, for the first time, Tess noticed that his thick mane of hair was brushed back from a forehead that had far too many lines for someone she knew to be only in his late thirties. He seemed tense. His grandmother said he worked too hard and worried too much. From everything Aunt Martha had told her about his behavior, Tess knew that Daniel Friday desperately needed to learn how to cut loose, enjoy life, smell a few roses.

She sighed. Too bad he lived in Pittsburgh. She wouldn't have minded taking him on as a project and tutoring him in the finer points of elementary rose smelling. No, she thought with a smug inner grin, she wouldn't have minded at all. Daniel Friday had real potential.

"I think they plan to be back this evening, but with those two, you never can tell," Tess said. "They may decide to stop at Delta Downs to check out Pirate's Pleasure."

"Delta Downs? Is that what I think it is?"

"It's a racetrack in Louisiana, just across the state line."

He scowled. "My God, what business does an eighty-year-old woman have at a racetrack? And can you tell me why the hell she moved out of that very exclusive retirement home that she was so anxious to move to, or why she now wants to buy an RV?"

"An RV?" Tess bit back a chuckle. "It must be for the top secret project."

"Top secret project? What top secret project? Has Gram become senile?"

Tess burst out laughing. "Far from it. She and Aunt Olivia are both in full possession of all their faculties and having the time of their lives. They were girlhood friends, you know. I can see I need to explain a few things to you, but I've got to get the Mermaidmobile stocked so Becky can go out on her rounds."

"Mermaidmobile? Who's Becky?"

"She manages Mermaid, a frozen yogurt shop downtown, but she had an important errand to run this morning, so I promised to have the delivery wagon ready when she got back. It seems that all the employees picked today to have emergencies, and I'm elected to help out." She chewed on her lip for a moment, then said, "I feel just awful about not being able to entertain you until Aunt Olivia and your grandmother get home. Any other day, it wouldn't be a problem, but—"

"Don't concern yourself." He answered politely, but he was frowning. "I'll find a hotel room until—"

"Don't be silly." She hooked his arm with hers and took off at a fast clip up the pier. When they were on the boulevard, she said, "You'll go to our place and make yourself at home until you can see your grandmother. Do you have a car?" He nodded. "Ivan should be back from fishing soon, and he would love to try one of his new masterpieces on you for lunch. I think we're into shrimp dishes now."

"Who's Ivan?" Daniel asked. "The cook?"

Tess pursed her lips to keep from laughing. Ivan would pop a blood vessel if he knew someone had referred to him as a "cook." Cocking her head, Tess pondered the question. "No, not exactly. How do I explain Ivan Petkov?"

"Petkov? Is he Russian?"

Tess shook her head. "Bulgarian originally. American now. He's a friend of Aunt Olivia's, though for thirty years, he's been trying to make her more than a friend. He's an internationally-known chef who comes to visit now and then, sometimes for a few days, sometimes for a few years."

"*Years?*"

Tess laughed at his incredulous expression. "Sometimes."

"How long has this visit been?"

"Almost two years so far. He came when my aunt fell and broke her hip. Ivan and I arrived the same day. After she recovered, he stayed on to write a cookbook."

"And you?"

She shrugged. "I just stayed."

She strode toward her car, a creamy-yellow junkyard hybrid she called Buttercup. As she tossed her bagpipe in the back seat, she saw Dan do a double take, and she smiled. Buttercup affected a lot of people that way—it was great advertisement for Custom Conversions, the body shop and garage she owned with Luis Garza.

He frowned at the front of the car, walked around and frowned at the rear. "What *is* this thing?"

She patted the fender. "Buttercup is a Custom Conversion. Pretty, isn't she? Before Luis found her at the junkyard and fixed her up, she was a rusty green Volkswagen beetle. After he overhauled the engine, he added a scaled-down Rolls-Royce grille, a continental tire kit to the back, wire wheels, and" —she brandished her hand in an exaggerated presentation—"*voilà* . . . a new incarnation."

"Interesting," Daniel said.

As her eyes slid over the conservative navy blazer, the gray slacks, and the correct silk tie, Tess fought a smile. Although he reminded her a little of Clint Eastwood before he lost his hair, she knew he was no "Dirty Harry." Daniel Friday's image was corporate establishment to the core. What had happened to the sexy, playful man she had glimpsed earlier? It was somewhere under all that Brooks Brothers baloney. He needed loosening up in a bad way. And she was just the person to tweak his buttoned-down sensibilities.

"Which translates," she said with a wry twist of her lips, "to '*I* wouldn't be caught dead driving such a thing.' "

"Now, I didn't say that."

She laughed. "You didn't have to. I'll bet you drive a Mercedes." She squinted at him for a moment. "Brown."

"Gray."

"Close enough."

He seemed surprised. "How did you know?"

"Lucky guess." She could spot the type at fifty paces. Her old Mercedes had been beige. She much preferred Buttercup.

"I know you're in a hurry, but could you explain Gram's sudden interest in racetracks and RVs? I'm concerned."

"Well, Pirate's Pleasure is a racehorse Aunt Olivia and Aunt Martha want to buy, and—"

"A racehorse?" The words erupted from him. Looking at her with a pained expression as if his shorts were too tight, he mashed his fingers against the tail of his silk tie. "What in the hell would two old ladies do with a racehorse?"

If he was upset about the racehorse, he'd probably blow a gasket over the RV and the treasure-hunting scheme. She'd wait and let his grandmother explain that one. Tess glanced down at her watch.

"Yikes, it's almost nine o'clock. Becky will kill me if the delivery wagon isn't ready." Giving him a bright smile, she scrambled into the car and fluttered her fingers. "Bye. I've got to run. Be sure and make yourself at home. I'll see you later," she called out as she roared away from the curb.

Just as Janice and Sue came in to work the evening shift at the Mermaid, Ivan phoned. He reported that Dan was reading in the study, and that Hook and the ladies had phoned from Louisiana. Thrilled to hear that Dan was in town, they promised to be back in time for dinner. Tess peeled off her stained apron and hurried to the house on Broadway.

After she had bathed, Tess slipped on a long tube dress slit from left ankle to knee and turned the convertible turtleneck into an off-the-shoulder band. Though she considered this cotton knit dress one of her most comfortable, the bold purple and teal-swirled fabric also hugged every curve of her body. And a good body it was, she admitted as she surveyed herself critically in the full-length mirror. Especially since she'd stopped spending her days behind a desk.

She spritzed a bit of Opium on her throat and brushed her short hair back into full gleaming waves. She even took time to add a touch of exotic eye shadow and a dash of lipstick. She told herself it wasn't for Daniel Friday, but, as she studied her reflection in the mirror, she kept trying to picture herself in his eyes. Her chin lifted and her shoulders drew back just a tad.

With a wry smile, she cocked an eyebrow and said, "Maybe I'll give you a little something to remember on those cold nights in Pittsburgh, Mr. Friday."

She added a few bangle bracelets, and dangling peacock feather earrings that brushed against her bare skin, then slipped into Moroccan sandals and went downstairs.

Ivan and Dan were having drinks in the large formal drawing room. Tess entered the room and smiled as she listened to the booming voice of the older man regaling Dan with one of his exploits. Ivan, who dearly loved a fresh audience, was perched on the edge of a gilt chair, gesturing broadly. He looked totally out of place in the high-ceilinged room with its Aubusson carpet, gold chandelier, and rococo revival furniture. The beefy Bulgarian wore a Greek fisherman's sweater, his latest sartorial passion, stretched over his thick chest.

Dan, in his navy blazer, seemed more comfortable on the elaborately carved settee where he sat listening politely to Ivan's tale. He had on a fresh shirt and another conservative tie, the spares, no doubt, which every good executive carried in his trusty leather briefcase. Before either of the men was aware of her presence, she took a moment to study Dan and wondered what he would look like in a fisherman's sweater with that fantastic hair of his a little mussed. Damned good, she suspected.

"Have another Shrimp Puff Olé," Ivan said as he thrust the silver tray at Daniel. When Dan declined, Ivan drew his shaggy brows together and asked, "Too spicy, you think?" Before he received an answer, Ivan caught sight of Tess. "Ah, my lovely Tess, come taste my shrimp puffs. I make a new creation from the beautiful shrimps I catch today with my own hands. Here," he boomed, thrusting the tray toward her. "Taste and tell me what you think."

Tess winked at Dan, who had stood when she entered, and popped one of the delicate golden morsels in her mouth. As she chewed and swallowed, her eyes widened and glazed with tears. "Good Lord, Ivan," she gasped.

"A little too hot maybe?"

"A *little* hot? It would take the hair off a dog."

Ivan roared with laughter. "Just like my Olivia. She never spares my feelings when I make a disaster. I will put these down the disposal." He started out the door, tray in hand. "Take the hair off a dog. I like that." His robust laughter echoed behind as he left.

"Is he always so . . ."

"Gregarious? Blustery? Larger-than-life?" Tess supplied, laughing. "Always. But he's really a dear, a teddy bear underneath all that bravado." With Dan following, she crossed to the drink cart and mixed a wine spritzer for herself. "He rarely ever prepares anything that isn't delicious, but when he has a failure, it's a doozy. How many of those fireballs did he foist off on you?"

"I only had a couple."

"And you managed to keep a straight face? You must have an insulated digestive system."

"I think the Scotch dulled the pain." He laughed

and Tess was glad to see the more relaxed side of him peeking through.

He seemed a little looser this evening, Tess thought. She sipped her spritzer and assessed the tall man beside her with frank admiration. Oh, he had a long way to go before all the starch was out of his collar, but the blue-gray eyes perusing her were a bit less strained, the frown lines softer.

"You look lovely this evening. I like your plumage." His hand rested on her bare shoulder as his finger ruffled the edge of her feathered earring.

The sensation of his skin on hers, the message in his eyes, made the hairs on the side of her neck stand up, and the drink in her mouth turned to warm foam. And her silly knees started doing their own thing. Part of her wanted to purr and rub her cheek against his hand; the rest of her wanted to offer her other shoulder to be stroked. It was a darned shame he lived half a country away. She had a feeling about staid Daniel Friday. A powerful feeling.

She swallowed. "Thanks," she said, stepping out of his reach before she became addicted to his touch. How could a man affect her so? She'd been engaged to David Lloyd for nearly three years, and not once had her knees wobbled or the hairs on her neck prickled. "What kind of business are you in back in Pittsburgh?"

"Have you ever heard of Friday Elevators?"

"Of course." She started to say that, until two years ago, she could have quoted from their prospectus, or she could have recalled that the company had almost gone under some years ago but had shown a steady growth for about the last ten. Instead, she bit her lip.

"You're not going to say anything about business being up and down, are you?"

Tess laughed. "No, do you get that a lot?"

"All the time."

Ivan lumbered in with another tray, which Dan eyed suspiciously, "No, no." The chef waved a massive hand. "No more jalapeño juice. Only a little cream cheese with toasted almonds and very delicate herbs. Delicious, I promise. And the dinner I fix tonight, *ahhh*. If Hook doesn't get my Olivia back to taste it, I'll skewer that big ox. They should be home by now. Do you think they have trouble? Ach," he said, slapping his forehead with the heel of his hand, "I should never have trusted my love's safekeeping to that criminal."

"Now Ivan," Tess said, "you know that Hook would guard the ladies with his life."

"So you say, but I"—he patted his chest—"Ivan Petkov, say: Never trust a man with a gold tooth."

Noticing Dan's frown, Tess said, "Don't mind Ivan. He and Hook have been feuding for fifteen years. Hook is completely reliable and devoted to my aunt."

"Bah! He fools her to keep from going back to prison."

Daniel choked on his Scotch. *"Prison?"* He could feel new bile added to the fire piercing his gut. What kind of a madhouse was Gram living in? Maybe Kathy was right to be concerned.

Tess glared at Ivan, turned to Dan, and waved her hand dismissively. "Oh, that was a long time ago."

"What was he in prison for?" Dan tried to make his question casual, but he could feel the blood draining from his face.

Tess shrugged. "The first time he was in a bar fight. Manslaughter, I think it was. He was very young. Barely eighteen."

"The *first* time? There's more?"

She sighed and glared at Ivan again. "The second time was for armed robbery."

"My God!" Daniel felt a searing stab in his solar plexus and he clutched his hand to his stomach.

"We're home," a bass voice rumbled.

Daniel looked up to see his grandmother and another older woman. Standing in the doorway behind them, his slick bald head nearly touching the top of the frame, was a giant of a man. Built like a heavyweight wrestler with leg breaking on his mind, his bulk filled the opening. A thick scar creased his ebony cheek from the corner of his left eye to his chin. A gold front tooth winked from his broad grin.

"Gram—" Dan took two steps toward the short, gray-haired lady. A faint, shrill static filled his ears, and the world faded away.

Two

It was almost dawn. Tess sat beside the hospital bed watching clear liquid from a suspended bag drip slowly into the chamber which fed the long tube of Dan's IV. She'd been sitting in a straight chair, holding his hand, since he'd been transferred from intensive care the evening before.

Twice during the long night she had gotten up to go to the bathroom and ease the kinks from her body, but Dan had become so restless when her hand left his that she quickly settled back beside him.

"I'm here," she'd whispered, and when her fingers touched his once more, he'd squeezed her hand and slipped into a quiet sleep.

With her free hand, Tess took a sip of the coffee a thoughtful nurse had provided, and her eyes scanned the face that had become so familiar during her long vigil. She had memorized every dip and plane from tousled hair to strong jaw. Not even the little freckle at the corner of his lower lip had escaped her notice.

Though he still seemed pale beneath the sandy stubble of whiskers, his color was better. Sleep smoothed the furrows of his forehead and relaxed the hard set of his mouth.

In the past few hours a strange bond had grown between them. She felt it, the strength of it, the absolute rightness of it, deep within her. A fierce possessiveness tugged at her heart and swelled her throat. Daniel Friday was hers. She knew it as surely as she knew the sun would rise over the Gulf of Mexico. Fate, with a little push from Aunt Martha, had brought him to Galveston, to her. He needed to recapture old dreams and to learn the meaning of real joy. Knowing, accepting, Tess smiled. She's been waiting for someone like Dan for a long time. Though she suspected he would rather die than admit it, he needed someone like her. No, he needed *her*.

Dan's eyelids fluttered open. He blinked, frowned, and looked at her. "Tess?"

"Good morning," she said.

"Morning." The husky reply was an automatic response as he continued to frown at his surroundings. "I thought I dreamed you," he murmured, then licked his lips. "My mouth is so dry."

She helped him take a sip of water. "Feeling a little disoriented?" He nodded. "You're in John Sealy Hospital in Galveston. You've been very ill."

His eyebrows came together. "What are you talking about? I'm *never* sick." His words were slurred from the aftereffects of the medication. "And I haven't been in a hospital since I had my appendix out when I was twelve. What happened?"

"You fainted and—"

"Fainted?" His indignation woke him up.

Tess tried to keep the amusement from her voice.

"Sorry, you *passed out* in our living room. Luckily, a doctor who lives next door was home. Dr. Ed—Ed Shafer, he's an internist—called an ambulance. Things were shaky for a while, but you're going to be just fine." She patted his hand.

"What was wrong with me?"

"A gastric ulcer."

"An *ulcer*?"

She nodded. "A bad one."

"Good God!" He looked chagrined. "What time is it?"

Tess turned the hand he still held to look at her watch. "It's six forty-three in the morning."

Dan withdrew his hand and started to get up. "I've got to get out of here."

"Whoa, tiger." Tess pressed his shoulders back on the bed and motioned toward the IV with her head. "You're not going anywhere until the doctor says so. You're still hooked up and as weak as a newborn."

"I've got to get back to Pittsburgh."

"What's so wonderful about Pittsburgh? I've been there a couple of times, and, frankly, I think Galveston is much better for your health."

Straining against her hold, he scowled and said as if speaking to a child, "I have an important meeting scheduled with the board of directors. It's crucial that I attend."

Tess pursed her lips and slowly shook her head. "The meeting was day before yesterday. Kathy said to tell you that she took charge and everything went fine."

He slumped against the pillow and threaded his fingers through his hair. "My God, what day is it? How long have I been here?"

"It's Wednesday, and you've been here almost four

days. The first three days you were in intensive care. They moved you out late yesterday afternoon. Dan, you've really been very ill."

"Obviously I'm better now. Where are my clothes? I've got to get back to work."

"Not unless you're anxious to die," a gruff voice said from the doorway. A stocky, balding man with a stethoscope in the pocket of his white coat walked into the room.

Tess offered him a bright smile, got up, and pecked him on the cheek. "Good morning, Dr. Ed." To Dan she said, "This is Dr. Ed Shafer, our neighbor who saved your life. He's head of the internal medicine faculty at the University of Texas Medical Branch. If you had to get sick, you picked a good place for it. We have one of the finest health care facilities in the country."

"I'll remember that," Dan grumbled at her. "Dr. Shafer, I appreciate your care. Now, when may I get out of here? I have a company to run."

The doctor pulled another chair close to the bed and sat down. "Mr. Friday, I believe we need to talk about your plans. You were unconscious when we brought you in Saturday night, so I talked to several people in an effort to obtain your medical history— including your physician in Pittsburgh, who I understand hasn't seen you in four years. Your grandmother and your sister both told me the same thing: they said you were killing yourself running that company of yours. They may be right. You have gastritis and a severe gastric ulcer. I can't emphasize the seriousness of your condition enough. The kind of stress you've subjected yourself to can be fatal."

Daniel looked incredulous. "I've never heard of anyone dying from an ulcer."

"Believe me, it happens. Especially with severe gastric ulcers like yours."

"What do you recommend? Surgery? Medication? A special diet?"

"Surgery is not indicated at this time. Medication, a special diet, yes. But more important than that is rest and a complete change in life-style. I would suggest that you take off three months, six months—a year would be best—and forget about your business. Go off to an island somewhere, lie in a hammock in the sun, and watch the tide come in."

"Dr. Shafer, I can't take that kind of time away from the company. It's out of the question. People depend on me."

The doctor rose. "Then, Mr. Friday, you should get your affairs in order and select your pallbearers." He turned and left the room.

Stunned by the doctor's parting salvo, Daniel stared at the ceiling. His hand closed automatically over the fine-boned one that was offered. Was his condition as serious as Dr. Shafer had painted it, or was he using scare tactics to . . . to what? Why should the man lie?

Could Daniel afford to be away from the company for six months or a year? As vice president, the entire load would fall on Kathy. Could his baby sister handle it? Even though she was always complaining about his methods, lecturing him about delegating authority, badgering him to give her more responsibility, he'd always done everything he could to protect her and make things easier for her. Lord, he couldn't burden her with the ordeal of running Friday Elevators for even three months. He wouldn't wish that fate on the devil himself, much less the sister he loved.

Yet, if things were as serious as the doctor claimed, what were his options? Ted, his younger brother, was a promising playwright; all he knew about the business was that its stock's dividends kept him afloat in these early, lean years of his career. If Daniel died, the responsibility would be dumped on Kathy permanently. He shuddered at the thought of her having to deal with the hell he'd endured over the past twelve years.

At least Kathy was older than Daniel had been when the task of rebuilding the company that was near bankruptcy had fallen on his shoulders. He had just received his degree in architecture and had accepted a plum job with an outstanding firm. When his father died, he had abandoned his dream to pull the business out of the red. It had been a nightmare; it was still a nightmare, but the security of his family had always come first and, as the oldest son, the responsibility was his.

Certainly, with a Master's in business management, Kathy was better prepared to run a business than he'd been. Perhaps she could manage Friday Elevators for a few weeks.

A month. He'd give himself a month. If he called the office every day and moved Chuck Stanley in as Kathy's assistant, maybe she could keep things going for that long. It seemed there was no other choice.

Strangely, Daniel felt relieved.

"But where am I going to find an island and a hammock?" he mused aloud.

"Galveston is an island," Tess said, a slow grin breaking across her face. "And I think there's a hammock stashed somewhere in the garage. You can stay with us."

His frown returned. "I can't stay with you."

"And why not? We have lots of room. It's perfect. Aunt Martha will love it. She needs someone to fuss over." Tess didn't add that his staying in Galveston would be the answer to her own prayers.

Dan turned on his corporate persona full force. "It's out of the question. I'll buy Gram a condo in Florida and she can fuss over me there."

"Silliest thing I ever heard." Tess gave s dismissive wave of her hand as someone tapped on the door.

A head with a cap of white curls popped around the door. Martha Craven, Dan's short, slightly plump grandmother fluttered into the hospital room and dropped a kiss on his cheek. "Why such a scowl, Danny? Aren't you feeling better? Dr. Ed said—"

His scowl deepened. "I'm feeling fine, Gram."

"We were just discussing Dan's staying in Galveston while he recuperates," Tess explained. "I've told him we'd love to have him."

Martha clapped her hands together. "Oh, that's a wonderful idea. There's plenty of room and we can all take care of you. And when you're feeling better, we can buy the RV—I've had my eye on a Winnebago— and you can go treasure hunting with us."

Dan looked at her incredulously. "*Treasure hunting?* Are you serious?"

"Oops," a blue-veined hand went to her mouth. "I'm not supposed to talk about it—Olivia says we have to keep it quiet or someone will try to beat us to it—but since you're family, I'm sure it's all right." Her voice dropped to a whisper. "It's part of Jean Laffite's booty. He once lived on this very island. We have a map and all sorts of directions from an old journal. They really belong to Olivia and Tess, but since I found them when I was working on the genealogy, they're insisting that I get a share. If we find the treasure, Tess can have her house and Olivia and I can have our racehorse." She clapped her hands together. "Isn't it a gas?"

Daniel frowned. *A gas?* Had his very proper grandmother said "a gas"? Had the entire world gone crazy? If she wasn't senile, then something very peculiar was going on in that household. Treasure hunts and racehorses and convicts and bizarre little cars named Buttercup. The whole bunch of them was strange. Even if he was mightily attracted to Tess Cameron, he had to admit that she was odd too. He'd feel better if his grandmother were somewhere else. "How about Hawaii?"

Martha looked puzzled. "What about Hawaii?"

"Would you like a condo in Hawaii?"

"Certainly not. I love Galveston. And you will too, Danny." She patted his hand. "You will too."

Daniel shook his head. It had been a hell of a day.

Early the next afternoon. Tess and her passenger pulled away from the hospital and headed toward the house on Broadway.

"I'm not sure this is a good idea," Daniel said.

"Of course it is. We have an empty guest cottage where you can have all the privacy you want, and everybody is delighted to have someone to fuss over. Aunt Olivia and your grandmother have dusted and plumped the pillows three times already this morning. And Ivan, poor man, is convinced that his shrimp puffs caused your attack, so he's conferred with the hospital dietitian and has been busy concocting gastronomic delights to tempt your palate. How many people have an internationally-known chef prepare their ulcer diets?"

"Very few, I suspect. But I don't want to be any trouble."

"Trouble? Are you kidding? You're going to learn very soon that the folks in this house only do what they enjoy. It's the secret to a long and happy life. 'Kick back, relax, and enjoy life' is our motto. We're going to teach you how. Hook already has the hammock up in the backyard."

"Hook, the ex-con? I'd almost forgotten about him. He was the last thing I remember seeing before I blacked out. Lord, he's a big, mean-looking customer. Are you sure he's safe to have around?"

Grinning as she watched Dan's discomfort, Tess said, "Positive. Hook is unique and extremely talented. Forget about his prison time. He's as gentle as a lamb. He was the first one to volunteer to donate blood for you, and since you matched, you now have a pint of him in you. You're blood brothers, so to speak."

She almost giggled at the expression that flashed over Dan's face. "I'll have to thank him," he said. "And thank you for the clothes and other things you brought to the hospital."

"No problem. We figured you'd need a few items until Kathy could get your own clothes shipped down here."

When Tess had seen the knit pullover in the window of the shop next to the Mermaid, she'd known it would be perfect for Dan. And it was. Its soft blue-gray color was the exact shade of his eyes and showed off his amazingly well-shaped shoulders and chest. She'd also bought several other items; it had been fun outfitting Dan for a new, more relaxed lifestyle.

Thinking he might be the pajama type, she even

bought pajamas. But they were not striped cotton with a collar and buttons down the front. The ones she bought were loden green silk with a deep V-necked top and easy-moving baggy pants pegged at the ankle.

When she'd started to select underwear, Tess had passed up the conservative styles and had chosen a half dozen pair of colorful briefs: everything from electric blue silk briefs to Italian mesh to a jersey camouflage. She'd tossed them all into the bag she'd packed to take to the hospital. She couldn't resist asking, "Did you like the underwear?"

"Who picked it out? I can't imagine Gram buying commando briefs."

"She didn't. I did." Tess stole a glance at him in time to see his lips slowly curl up in amusement.

"I see."

She turned her attention back to her driving and nibbled at her lip. For the first time, she was having second thoughts about all the stuff she'd bought that was now hanging in the closet and neatly stacked in chest drawers in the guest cottage. What if he didn't like it? What if he resented her selecting clothes for him?

"I'm sorry if you don't like the camouflage skivvies. I bought them, and all the others, as kind of a joke to cheer you up. Aunt Olivia says that drinking the water in Galveston always makes everybody crazy, and I drink eight glasses every day. If you'd prefer boxer shorts or plain old Fruit of the Loom cotton knit, I'll be happy to run down to—"

"Tess." He interrupted her babbling with a hand on the shoulder of her chartreuse jumpsuit. "The ones you bought are fine. Thanks." He squeezed her shoulder for emphasis. "Maybe I'll even model them for you sometime."

Was he only teasing or did he mean it? She'd never been the type to fantasize about seductively clad men, but a sudden image of Dan in nothing but a strip of pink Italian mesh with a bit of strategically placed nylon did peculiar things to her heartbeat. Of course he was teasing. Wasn't he? She swallowed and looked at him out of the corner of her eye. He was frowning and staring out the window.

Feigning a seductive tone and wiggling her eyebrows, Tess said, "I'll hold you to that, big guy." She managed to make him laugh as she pulled into the driveway of the redbrick mansion and tooted the horn.

The next few minutes passed in happy chaos as everybody in the house poured out to welcome Dan home from the hospital.

Daniel thought the bunch of them looked like the cast of an off-Broadway farce. Both older women, one tall, one nearly a head shorter, were dressed in sweatsuits and Reeboks. Martha wore a lavender outfit with her pearls, while Olivia was clad in bold black and white stripes. When she'd visited him briefly at the hospital, Olivia's hair had been tucked under some kind of a turban. He stared at it now. Held back with a black sweatband, it was flaming red and hung halfway down her back. Her eyelashes were at least an inch long and obviously fake. Both octogenarians beamed at him.

Dan's grandmother, her snow-white crop of curls tickling his chin, hugged him as if she hadn't seen him in years when, in fact, she'd spent several hours at his bedside only the day before.

"Oh, Danny, it's wonderful to have you home from that dreadful, sterile place." Martha Craven dabbed at her eyes with a lace-edged handkerchief she pulled from a pocket. "And all you've had to endure!" She hugged him again with a new rush of tears.

"Martha, don't carry on so or you'll get the hiccups again." Olivia Oates, who had turned eighty-one in January and was almost as slim and fully as tall as Tess, patted Dan's back. "Now, Daniel, you're welcome here for as long as we can persuade you to stay. You must think of this as your home. Our digs are your digs, so to speak. And you must call me Aunt Olivia, just as my Tess does." She patted his back again. "We're going to have you mellowed out and coasting in nothing flat."

His grandmother on one side and Olivia on the other ushered him toward the front porch, where Hook and Ivan stood waiting. Dan glanced back at Tess as if to say, "Save me from all this," but Tess only grinned and shrugged.

"I believe you already know Ivan," Olivia said to Daniel, "but you conked out the other night before you met Julius." She introduced him to the menacing black giant with the scar and the bald head. "Julius runs the household. Anything you need, let him know."

"Hook," the big man said in a bass voice, taking the hand that Daniel offered. "Call me Hook. Nobody but Miss Olivia calls me Julius."

His grin was so broad that it showed not only his gold front tooth but the star cutout decorating its surface. Daniel forced a smile and thanked him for the blood donation, but he wasn't convinced that anyone with Hook's history could be trusted with the family silver. Or with his grandmother.

Ivan Petkov bowed, his expression contrite. "Please accept my profuse apologies for the shrimp puffs. My heart is overwhelmed with grief for the pain they caused your stomach."

"Ivan—" Dan began.

"No, no." Ivan held up both beefy hands. "Tess explains, but still I feel remorse for my idiocy. You must let me make amends. I work my fingers to the bone to devise tempting dishes for your diet. Not one iota will I deviate from the hospital's list. Come into my kitchen and taste the eggnog I have created for you. Ah, fantastic! I think I shall write a new cookbook. I shall dedicate it to you."

Ivan would not be satisfied until the entire assemblage followed him back to the large kitchen and tasted his Eggnog Friday. Daniel even took a tentative sip to humor the Bulgarian, but despite the welcome—and Tess—he was trying to figure out a way to extract his grandmother from this loony bin.

"The touch of almond extract is the secret." Ivan slapped Daniel's back. "Delicious, is it not?" When Daniel agreed, the blustery chef said, "I leave a pitcher in the refrigerator here in the kitchen and another in the small one in your cottage. You must drink a glass every two hours for the good of your stomach. And we have dinner early. Not that hospital food. Bah! I fix—"

"Ivan, cool it." Olivia shot him a quelling glance. "Daniel needs rest, a little peace and quiet, not a recitation of your concoctions." When Ivan hung his head, she patted him on the shoulder. "You know we're all appreciative of your very great talents."

Ivan smiled and kissed her hand. Three times.

Olivia sighed and turned to Daniel. "You'll have to forgive us if we all seem a little overzealous. Things will quiet down in a few minutes. Martha, Hook, Ivan, and I are going to check out a new art exhibit this afternoon. We'll leave Tess to get you settled in."

Martha looked startled. "But Olivia—"

"You'll see Daniel at dinner," Olivia said to her friend, and she herded the others out of the kitchen, leaving only Daniel and Tess behind.

As the four trooped out, Daniel leaned against the big butcher block, sipping his eggnog and shaking his head. "You know," he said when he noticed Tess watching him, "this stuff *is* good."

Tess burst out laughing. "I should hope so. Ivan could name his own salary at any one of the top-rated hotels or restaurants in the country."

"Then why is he here?"

"Because he adores my aunt. He was distraught when she fell and broke her hip. I doubt he'll ever leave again. She saved his life after he escaped from Bulgaria about thirty years ago. Ivan's been begging her to marry him ever since."

"Why doesn't she?"

"She says it's because he's twenty years younger than she is, but I suspect there's another reason as well."

Daniel drank the last of his eggnog and set the glass down. "Which is?"

"She was very much in love with a man when she was in her twenties. They were engaged and planned to be married in a double wedding ceremony with her twin sister, my grandmother. Unfortunately, he was killed."

"And she never married?"

Tess shook her head. "My family has an unusual history. If a woman finds love, it's only once and it's fierce. If that's lost . . ." She shrugged. "Enough of that. You must be tired. Come on, I'll show you to the cottage."

Daniel followed her to the hallway, glancing at the portraits as he went. He stopped in front of one, obviously very old, and stepped back to get a better look at it. "Who is this imposing fellow? One of your ancestors?"

Tess laughed. "Yes. He was my great-great-grand-father, Marsh Prophet, Captain Marsh Prophet of the Texas Rangers before he met and married my great-great-grandmother Acasia. Casey, she was called. This is her portrait." Tess pointed to the painting next to the first.

"Very beautiful," Dan said glancing back and forth between Tess and the painting of her ancestor. "You look a little like her."

Tess was warmed by his words. Did he think she was beautiful? She'd never considered herself so, but all of a sudden it became important that Dan find her attractive. "Do you really think so?"

His eyes locked with hers. "I do. You're a lovely woman, Tess." He touched her cheek with the back of his fingers. "Warm, alive, alluring. Very alluring." His knuckles slid along the side of her face, barely grazing the skin. The tip of his index finger traced the contour of her lips. "And like the siren's song, you tempt me. I think you may be a little dangerous."

Something happened to her chest. She couldn't breathe. She felt dolphins playing in her stomach and fireflies lighting up her brain. "You do?" Her voice seemed even hoarser than usual.

"I do."

For a moment she thought he was going to kiss her, then he dropped his hand and turned to the portraits again. Why had he stopped? She wouldn't have minded. After all, he was hers already. They belonged together. He just didn't know it yet.

• • •

"Damn!" Daniel slammed the phone down. "Hard-headed little witch," he muttered as someone tapped on the door. "Come in," he growled.

Martha Craven fluttered into the living room of the cottage. "Am I interrupting something?"

Struggling to calm his temper, he said, "No, Gram."

His tiny grandmother dropped a kiss on his cheek. "Danny," she said, smoothing his hair from his forehead, "something has upset you. You looked much better at breakfast this morning. What happened?"

"I just talked to Kathy. Or at least I tried to talk to Kathy. She informed me that she's instructed *her* secretary not to take any more calls from me. Until today I thought Ruth was *my* secretary."

"Oh, is that all?" Martha Craven pursed her lips and her blue eyes twinkled as she settled on the sofa beside him. She laced her fingers together in her lap. "I thought it was something serious."

"Serious? It's damned serious! How am I supposed to keep the company afloat if I can't have access to it? I'm the president, for God's sake!"

"Now, dear." Gram leaned over and patted his hand. "Don't get in a stew. Remember your ulcer. Dr. Shafer said that you were to stay away from the stresses of the company. Kathy's not accepting your calls for your own good. She wants you to be well and happy. She can handle the business just fine. I have every confidence in her."

Daniel scowled, stood up, and raked his fingers through his hair. "I've got to get back to Pittsburgh right away."

"Why?"

"Because," he said with measured words, "our family and a lot of other families depend on Friday Elevators. Have you forgotten that you invested your entire fortune in the company to help save it after Dad was sick for so long?"

"Danny, your health is more important to us than money."

"Gram, I'm the president and I'm responsible."

Martha Craven sighed and worried the pearls at her lace collar. "No, you're not."

"Of course I'm responsible. You can't expect Kathy—"

"Danny, you're not the president."

Daniel's eyes narrowed. "What do you mean?"

"The board of directors made Kathy acting president for a three-month period. At that time, they'll reevaluate the situation, including your health and your wishes."

"The board of directors? What are you talking about, Gram? With my stock and yours and Ted's proxies, I control the board of directors."

Gram fidgeted as Daniel stared at her, awaiting her answer. "Teddy and I reassigned our proxies to Kathy." Her words were barely a whisper.

Daniel dropped his head and uttered an expletive that he was sure made his grandmother blush.

"It's only temporary," she assured him. "Until you're well again."

Shuddering as he sucked in a gulp of air, he sat down on the edge of the sofa. Elbows on his knees, he clamped his hands together and stared at the floor. Frustration, anger, and self-disgust played tag in his head. Never in his life had Daniel felt like such a useless piece of garbage. Damn his weak gut! He couldn't even take care of his family.

Three

His bare feet propped on an ottoman, his fingers laced across his middle, Dan sat slumped in an easy chair and stared at the wall. The baggy gray sweatpants and old Penn State jersey he wore had, like him, seen better days. He hadn't showered or shaved in two or three days, but he just didn't give a damn.

Outside, the sun was shining, but inside the cottage it could have been midnight. The blinds were closed, the drapes were shut, and not a single bulb burned to dispel the gloom. The darkness suited him just fine. He'd had a bellyful of sunshine and cheer from Gram and that whole crazy bunch she was mixed up with. They seemed to expect him to act as if nothing had happened.

But something had happened, and it gnawed at him like rats eating through litter in a back alley. Not only had his body betrayed him, but his family had betrayed him as well. Even Gram. Under the guise of "doing it for his own good," they had sneaked around behind his back and taken the presidency from him. That had hurt. Hurt badly. He could have handled things if they'd given him a chance.

He knew he'd acted like a bastard to everybody since he'd found out what his family had done. But he couldn't seem to help himself. He hated this feeling of uselessness. The pain and the anger festered in him like a septic sore.

Somebody knocked on the door. He ignored it.

"I know you're in there, Friday," Tess yelled. "Open the door."

Daniel raked his fingers through his hair. Hell, he didn't want to see anybody now. Especially Tess. Having her witness his shame rankled.

The banging grew louder. "If you don't open the door, I'll have Hook come break it down."

She probably would. He muttered a curse and heaved himself out of the chair. He unlocked the door and opened it a crack to order her to leave. But before he could make a sound, she shoved her way inside.

"It's like a cave in here," she said, setting down the tray she carried.

"I like it dark."

Tess ignored his comment. She marched around the room, throwing back curtains and opening blinds with a missionary zeal. When she'd finished, she turned and flicked her eyes over him from his bare feet to his favorite old sweatpants and ragged jersey that Kathy had sent with some other clothes.

She frowned. "You look awful."

He knew how he looked, but having her say it ripped at the tattered remnants of his pride. His gaze passed over the green drawstring pants she wore to the oversized pullover with a large handpainted lion on the front. "Thanks. And I see you're sporting your haute couture today."

Her chin lifted. "You don't have to be insulting. These are my work clothes."

He plucked the front of his jersey. "These are my work clothes, too. I'm practicing being a bum."

"You've succeeded. I brought your lunch." She picked up the tray and gestured toward the rattan dining table.

"I'm not hungry."

She pursed her lips and drew in a deep breath. "Dan, you have to eat properly or you'll never get well. Your grandmother is worried out of her mind."

He scowled. "I said I'm not hungry."

She was furious at this stubborn man who had so disrupted her household. Everyone had tried to be patient and understanding and appropriately sympathetic, but in the week he'd been here, Dan had become progressively more surly. He had rebuffed any offer of kindness and had finally holed up in the cottage, refusing even to join the family at mealtimes. Aunt Martha was crying and hiccupping; Ivan was beside himself; and Aunt Olivia, who never let anything bother her, was in bed with a migraine.

Sweet, gentle Hook had curled his gigantic hands into fists and said to Tess, "You handle that dude, or I will."

Hook was right. They had tiptoed around him long enough. The time had come for a different approach.

She shoved the tray against his midsection. "You're damned well going to eat this if I have to hold you down and force-feed you."

Daniel snatched the tray from her and hurled it

out the front door. When he turned back to glare at Tess, his eyes were narrowed.

She glared back at him. "Cute, Friday. Very cute. If you've got any ideas of tossing me out with your lunch, guess again. I've been taking karate lessons and I'm damned good." Fists on her hips, she ground out her words through clenched teeth. "What's the matter with you? You've been spoiling for a fight for days. Everybody has been trying to help you and you've been acting like a first-class jerk."

"I don't need any help from you or anybody. Get out of here and leave me alone," he roared.

"If you're so miserable here, why don't you go back to Pittsburgh?" she shouted.

"I'm not leaving my grandmother alone with a bunch of weirdos!"

"*Weirdos?* Who are you calling weirdos? *You're* the one who's weird. Those people," she enunciated, waving her hand toward the house, "are loving, caring human beings. One of them gave you his blood and has been toting trays out here so you won't starve!" Tess was in his face and punctuating every word with a jab in his chest. "Another one is distraught because you've been picking at your food. Poor Ivan spent two hours preparing the lunch you just pitched out in the yard! One of them—"

Dan grabbed her by the shoulders and ground his mouth against hers. It was not a kiss; it was an angry, bitter silencing. When Tess struggled to pull away, his hand captured the back of her head and held her lips to his.

His stubble scratched her face and her teeth were mashed against her lips. Yet even as he held her roughly, Tess could tell that he was holding back, leashing a seething inner fury. She ceased her struggles and stood still as a post.

After a few seconds, Dan thrust her away, turned, and muttered, "Damn!" He slapped the wall with his splayed left hand and, stiff-armed, leaned into it. His head dropped and his right hand curled into a fist. "God damn!" The fist drove into the Sheetrock and punched a jagged hole.

For a moment neither of them moved. Then Dan, his fist still buried up to his forearm, his head still down, said, "Get out of here."

"I'm not leaving."

"I'm sorry, Tess. I didn't mean to hurt you. I'm sorry."

Tears sprang to her eyes when she heard the agony in his voice. "You didn't hurt me. You're the one who's hurting, Dan. Want to talk about it?"

"No, I want you to leave."

"I'm not going anywhere." She stepped beside him. "Let me see your hand. I may need to put something on it."

"Lord, go away, Tess. Don't you know how humiliating this is for me?"

"What is humiliating? Acting like a jerk? Throwing a temper tantrum? Coming on to me like a Neanderthal? Getting booted out of the company because your family cares about you? Or," she said, her voice softening, "is it being human and needing help?" She put her hand on his forearm, which was covered with powdery plaster from the wall.

He didn't answer right away. When they came, his words were barely audible. "All of it."

"And you feel like a failure?" She felt his muscles tighten under her hand.

"Save the psychoanalysis."

Tess sighed. Why were men always so reluctant to admit to emotions? She suspected that Dan needed a good cry. It was nature's remedy for releasing pain, but he'd never capitulate to a few healthy tears. Men usually masked everything in anger and aggression.

She tugged at his arm. "Let me see your hand."

Dan withdrew his fist from the wall to reveal scrapes on his knuckles. "I'm sorry about the hole. I'll pay to have it repaired."

"You certainly will. Come in the bathroom and let me clean these scratches."

In the bathroom, Tess washed his hand with warm, soapy water and poured peroxide on the scraped skin. "There," she said, recapping the bottle, "that should do it."

She looked in the mirror and the reflection of Dan's gaze met hers. The anger had disappeared. His eyes were softer, filled with a gentler expression. The tiny room shrank. He turned her toward him and lifted her chin.

"Tess, I'm sorry if I hurt you earlier. I've wanted to kiss you since the first moment I saw you. I've thought about it every time I've seen you. I've even dreamed about it, but I never meant it to be like that. I wanted . . ." His thumb slid over the bottom curve of her lip.

Her breath caught and her eyes fixed on the little freckle at the corner of his mouth. "You wanted?"

He gave a rueful smile. "It doesn't matter."

She could feel the room shrinking more, and her knees were beginning to go weak. Every sense was attuned to the closeness of him as she stared, mesmerized, at that little freckle. "Why not?" Her voice was almost a whisper.

"I don't feel like much of a man anymore."

Her eyes rolled heavenward. "Oh, good grief!" Tess grabbed the back of his head, pulled his face to hers and planted a kiss on Dan Friday that would have unraveled his socks, if he'd been wearing any.

She arched her back and rubbed her breasts across his chest and plunged her tongue between his lips. He groaned as his arms came around her, gathering her body against his. His mouth moved over hers like a starving man at a feast, tasting, savoring, devouring.

Heat flashed between them like spontaneous combustion. Tess had never felt anything so potent, so overwhelming in her life. When his arm scooped her pelvis close to the juncture of his legs, she was shocked to find herself writhing against the hardness of him.

Gasping for breath, she pulled back and looked into his darkened eyes. His breathing was as ragged as hers. One eyebrow lifted and her gravelly voice was an octave deeper as she said, "Lord, Friday, you feel like a man to me."

His lips curved into a smile, the smile changed to a grin, and finally he threw back his head and laughed. "Tess Cameron, you're some kind of woman. Where have you been all my life?"

"Waiting for you," she said with a saucy grin. "You have exactly thirty minutes to stop feeling sorry for yourself, shave that mess off your face, and get dressed. I have work to do and I need a helper. You're elected."

When Tess came downstairs half an hour later, she found Dan sitting at the kitchen table and Ivan beaming.

"Daniel liked the potato soup I prepared so well," Ivan announced, "that he came in for a second helping."

She leaned against the counter and, with a slight twitch of her lips, said, "Oh, really?"

Daniel didn't glance up from his plate, but Tess could have sworn that she saw his shoulders shaking. Shoulders, she noted, nicely encased in the peach pullover she'd bought for him. With it he wore a pair of chinos and the deck shoes she'd chosen as well. When his spoon scraped the bottom of the bowl, he looked up and grinned. "My compliments, Ivan. I believe this tasted even better than the first."

Ivan's chest swelled noticeably.

Tess rolled her eyes but didn't give him away. "Are you ready?"

Dan stood. "Ready."

"Why don't we walk? It's a beautiful day and it's less than a dozen blocks to the Strand."

They went out the back door, and he stuck his hands in his pockets as they ambled along the street lined with a mixture of live oak, pecan, and palm trees. As they walked through the East End Historical District, Tess pointed out turn-of-the-century houses in various states of repair, typical of the Galveston she had come to love. Some, sporting flower boxes full of geraniums, had been restored to their former Victorian splendor. They were interspersed with others that had been ignored and were succumbing to the ravages of time and the salty island dampness.

Usually Tess reminisced about the houses and their colorful histories as she passed; today her attention was focused on the man who walked beside her. Since his outburst earlier, he seemed less morose, less hostile. Maybe it had been good for him to let out a little of the anger he'd been bottling up.

When he caught her watching him, he smiled. "What new adventure do you have planned today?"

"I promised Nancy Vaughn that I'd help hang paintings for this weekend's exhibition at the Sea Song Gallery. Are you any good with a hammer and nails?"

Dan looked affronted. "Are you kidding? You're looking at the first place winner of the fifth grade birdhouse building contest."

"That good, huh?"

"Actually, as I recall, it was a pretty sorry-looking birdhouse, but I slaved over it. I built it from scraps I scavenged from the building sites I was always hanging around and painted it with shoe polish. I thought it was grand until I got to school and saw the other entries. Beside them, mine looked rather pathetic."

"Yet you won first place?"

He nodded. "It was obvious to the judge, who was an architect, that the other kids' fathers had built theirs. He told me I'd done a fine job, pinned the blue ribbon to my shirt, and shook my hand. It was the proudest moment of my life. I think it was then I decided to be an architect. I still have the ribbon somewhere."

Tess felt a lump in her throat as he recounted the story. There was a poignancy to his words, a wistfulness to his gaze as he remembered the events of long ago. And it touched her. Beneath Dan's stoic facade she sensed both passion and sensitivity aching to be expressed—she'd glimpsed the potential a few times. Something deep inside her desperately wanted to draw him into her arms and hold him close, but she struggled against the urge.

Aunt Martha had told her about Dan's aborted dream to become an architect, but Tess suspected that with his pride, he wouldn't appreciate knowing that they had discussed intimate details of his life. From the things Aunt Martha had told her, it seemed that Dan was a very private person.

"But you never followed up on your interest in architecture?" she asked, hoping he would confide in her.

"I did. I have a degree in architecture. Graduated summa cum laude."

"Then why . . ."

"Why am I—correction—*was* I the president of Friday Elevators?" There was the faintest tinge of bitterness in his voice.

She nodded.

He shrugged. "Things happen. Priorities change." Dan stopped in front of a large old house that had once been a grand residence. He leaned against its magnificent cast-iron fence, now pocked and rusting from neglect, and stared at the vacant wooden structure that was on the verge of collapse. "How sad," he said. "It must have been beautiful in its day."

Knowing that Dan had closed the door to any more personal disclosures, Tess sighed and reminded herself that she must be patient. She leaned against the fence and turned her attention to the decaying two-story house with its ornate towers, curlicued cupola, and "For Sale" sign in front. Most of the windows were boarded up, and only raw lumber props kept the second floor's sagging portico from crashing down on its Greek Revival twin below.

"It was. I have pictures at home. As I recall, it was built in 1886 by one of Galveston's leading citizens.

Or rebuilt, I should say, when the two smaller houses that were joined together and enhanced. Looking at it now, it's hard to believe that it once housed a wealthy family who gave grand formal balls. Until it became uninhabitable a few years ago, it had declined to a rather shabby apartment house with wash hanging from the top gallery."

"Doesn't Galveston have a historical society to save wonderful houses like this one?"

"Of course," Tess said. "An excellent one, but the island is filled with magnificent old homes going to seed, some even listed in the National Registry. They do as much as they can, but finances are limited. This one survived the great hurricane and the grade-raising, but it can't survive neglect."

"The 'grade-raising'?"

"Galveston used to be much lower," Tess explained. "After the hurricane of 1900 killed thousands of people and almost leveled the town, the stalwart citizens who decided to stay built the seawall and raised the level of the island. Some of the buildings were jacked up and fill was put underneath. Others, like our house and this one, lost most of their basements. My ancestors, the Prophets, decided to fill in their ground floor—to turn it into the house's basement—rather than risk structural damage by raising the house. Our yard was originally three feet lower, and this one was about the same."

Dan shook his head and his face betrayed his pain as his gaze swept over the deteriorating, once-elegant residence. "Such a waste. It almost cries out to be saved. I wish there was something I could do. Once I considered—" His words trailed off as he turned abruptly from the house. "Hadn't we better be going if we're going to hang paintings?"

Tess waved a hand dismissively. "We have plenty of time." Cocking her head and narrowing her eyes as a thought occurred to her, she said, "Do you really like old houses?"

"Sure. Is that so strange? I told you I studied architecture."

"I guess I've always associated modern architects with split-level houses or those giant smoked-glass phallic symbols that spring up in the cities and rape the sky."

Dan laughed. "I take it you don't approve of skyscrapers?"

Tess made a derisive sound. "Hate them. Come on," she said, grabbing his hand. "I want to show you something special. It's only a couple of blocks out of the way. You'll love it."

He matched his long stride with hers as she took off down the intersection. "Where are we going now?"

"I'm going to show you my house."

"But I've seen your house. I'm staying there, remember?"

"That's Aunt Olivia's house. Oh, I suppose it's half mine since my grandmother left me her share, but I've never been comfortable with all those gilt chairs and gold chandeliers. I've always wanted something . . . bolder. Something with more personality. Character. The one I want to show you is going to be all mine. You've heard of 'The House of the Seven Gables'? Well, mine has *nine*."

A few minutes later they were standing in front of the strangest house Daniel had ever seen. No, this imposing structure was not a house, he thought as he studied it carefully. It was a small palace, a peculiar hybrid of Moorish and Victorian Gothic with a battlement tower and an assortment of dormers and elaborately sculpted gables along the gray slate-covered roof.

The shrubbery in the small front garden area was badly overgrown, and tangles of vines almost covered the iron fence. More vines climbed upward through the dilapidated storm shutters, crawled over boarded windows, and clung to the rusticated cement stucco of the walls.

It certainly had character. But for the life of him, Daniel couldn't decide if this complexity of voluptuously carved corbels, lintels, and cornices was ugly or beautiful.

Until he glanced at Tess.

She was gazing up at the pseudo-stone house as if transfixed. Her lovely lips were curled into one of those smiles that made him want to follow her like a lapdog. She glowed.

"Isn't it magnificent?" Her husky voice curled around him and drew him into the magic that seemed to surround her like an aura.

"Magnificent," he said, not taking his eyes off her. Anything that could spark such fire in her eyes, such a rapt expression on her face, must be beautiful.

His gaze swept over her from the shock of full dark hair to the rubber soles of her leather sport shoes, then zeroed in on the green glass eyes of the lion painted on the front of her shirt. One of the emerald eyes, which caught the sun and glittered with her every breath, rested just above the crest of her right breast. It fascinated him, teased him, tempted him to reach out and touch it.

Its shimmer increased and he looked up to find her watching him. Her lips parted; her eyes seemed to smolder, to sear right through to his core. Sensuality pulsated from her lithe body, wrapped around him, and tugged at him with invisible fingers.

He took a step toward her. Then another. Oblivious to everything except Tess Cameron, he would have taken her in his arms if a van hadn't pulled alongside of them at that moment.

A middle-aged woman poked her head out the window. "Excuse me. Which way to the Railroad Museum?"

The moment was lost.

Daniel wanted to curse.

Tess turned to the woman and smiled. "Straight ahead for seven blocks. Turn left on Strand and you'll run right into it."

"Thanks," the woman said, waving as the van drove away.

Tess stood on the curb and returned the wave. It was not so much a friendly gesture as an opportunity to gather her wits and give her heart time to slow down. One look from the depths of Dan Friday's blue-gray eyes and she had almost attacked him in the middle of the East End Historical District at two o'clock in the afternoon.

If she'd ever had any doubt about Dan's potential for passion, it was gone now. She felt as if she'd been inside a bottle rocket. She took a deep breath, puffed her cheeks and blew it out.

Pasting a bright smile on her face, Tess turned and said, "Would you like a look inside? I have a key."

Not waiting for an answer, she grabbed his hand and dragged him past the "For Sale" sign and up the eighteen steps to the front entry. Her fingers were trembling so badly that even after three stabs at it, she couldn't get the key in the lock.

Dan took the key from her and opened it on the first try. When he held the door for her, she flounced past him, irked to no end that his hands were steady. Obviously she hadn't had the effect on him that he had had on her.

"It's pretty grim inside," she said, her voice echoing through the darkened house. "At some time or another it was chopped up into apartments. Walls will have to be knocked out and the entire inside redone, but I think it's structurally sound. Isn't that flowered wallpaper ghastly?" She detoured around some mouse droppings. "Looks like I'll need an exterminator, too."

"Mmmm." Dan stepped over a rotting section of the floor and followed her through the rooms.

"Isn't the staircase fantastic? It only needs a couple of spindles replaced. Stripped and refinished, it will be beautiful. And the fireplaces are all in fairly good shape. Italian marble, most of them. Can you imagine how beautiful it can be with everything done in bright colors and a comfortable eclectic look? I want Russian samovars and Persian rugs and big cushy couches. Can you imagine the possibilities?"

Her enthusiasm was infectious. Daniel grinned. "Yes, I believe I can."

"Of course you can. I forgot you're an architect." Her eyes widened. "I have an idea. Would you help me restore it?"

His grin widened. "For room and board?"

"If you like, but I'll be happy to pay your fee."

Daniel crammed his hands in his pockets and looked around. It would be a challenge. An exciting one. Then he frowned. "Most of the interior would have to be gutted. I'm sure it would need new wiring and new plumbing. Do you have any idea how expensive such a project would be?"

Tess shrugged. "I figure that the cost of the house, restoration, and refurnishing would be about a million—less the five thousand dollars earnest money I've put down to hold it for sixty days."

Dan's eyebrows raised. "And you can afford to lay out that much cash?"

She laughed. "Hardly. Although I did very well when I quit my job and got out of the stock market after I came to Galveston, most of the capital is invested in my businesses."

"Your businesses? I thought you just worked part time at the Mermaid. What happened to 'kick back and enjoy life'?"

"Oh, I did. I do. I'm a lazy entrepreneur. When I decided to stay after Aunt Olivia broke her hip, I planned to do nothing more than enjoy all the things I'd never had time for before. But I love Galveston and I wanted to do my part to help restore the grand old dame to at least a part of her former glory." She leaned against the black walnut banister and her hand absently stroked the fine, neglected wood. "So I bought a half block of the Strand and provided the cash for my partners' businesses. They're excellent investments like the Mermaid, Sea Song Gallery, a couple of boutiques. And, though it's not on the Strand, Luis's Custom Conversions. My partners in each business provide the skills and management in exchange for forty-nine percent of the profits. I simply lend a hand now and then for fun.

She looked him straight in the eye. "I've had my fill of the fast-paced, nose-to-the-grindstone life. When I moved to Galveston, Dan, I was plagued with headaches and backaches and neckaches. I didn't even know I'd been clenching my teeth for years. I had to wear a special splint in my mouth for months to get my jaw back to normal. Now my biggest worry is hanging a few paintings or finding a substitute driver for the Mermaid's delivery wagon."

Tess watched his reaction carefully, hoping he would ask her more, hoping he would see the parallel between her former life and his. Apparently it went past him. He acknowledged her disclosure with only a "Hmmm."

"Do you plan to get a million dollars' credit?" he asked. "That's a big commitment for someone who doesn't want any worries."

She slowly shook her head. "Nope. No loan."

"Then how do you plan to pay for all this?" He looked around the dirty, decaying rooms. "With buried treasure?"

She ignored his sarcastic comment and a big grin spread over her face. "Exactly."

Four

Dan looked at Tess as if she'd lost her mind. "I can't believe you're serious. Are you talking about the same screwball scheme that Gram was? I thought you were just humoring an old lady's fantasies."

"I'm perfectly serious. Aunt Martha told you we have Jean Laffite's map and directions from—"

He gave a derisive snort. "A treasure map? Good God, Tess, that's one of the oldest cons on earth. Out of all that assortment of oddballs, I was beginning to think that *you*, at least, had some sense." His eyes narrowed. "How much did you pay for this map?"

Fighting the urge to sock him right in the middle of his gorgeous Roman nose, Tess ground her teeth together. How could she be about to throw herself in his arms one minute and be tempted to brain him the next?

"Not . . . one . . . penny. Give me *some* credit, Friday. I didn't just fall off a turnip truck." She wheeled and stomped out of the house with Dan close behind her.

After she locked the door, they walked on toward the Strand without exchanging one word. It was Dan who finally broke the silence.

"Tess, I apologize. Why don't you tell me about the map."

Still stinging from his comments, she glanced over at him, trying to assess his motives. Was he truly interested or was he looking for more ammunition to debunk their plans? He looked innocent enough, but she was sick and tired of hearing him bad-mouth the people she loved.

"It appears to me, Daniel Friday, that you have a very bad habit of jumping to all sorts of erroneous conclusions. Are you really the pompous, self-righteous, crepe-hanger you seem to be, or have *I* misinterpreted your behavior?" She smiled sweetly.

Dan chuckled at her set down. "I suppose I have been acting like a condescending . . . jerk. I usually wait until I have all the facts before I make decisions. About situations and people. I'm honestly sorry, Tess. My only excuse it that I've been under a lot of stress."

She cocked an eyebrow. "Haven't we all?"

He grinned. "Why do I get the impression that I'm the cause of it?"

"If the shoe fits . . ."

He laughed. "Will you forgive me if I promise to try to do better?"

Tess sniffed. "I tentatively accept your tentative apology."

"Fair enough." He hooked her arm in his as they walked. "Now will you tell me about the map?"

"Maybe later." It was not in her nature to hold a

grudge, but Tess figured it would do Dan good to wonder a while longer. "You might be interested in this street," she said as they stopped at an intersection. "This part has some lovely old homes, but a few blocks west used to be one of the South's most famous red-light districts. It was originally named Avenue E, but it's better known as Post office Street."

His brows went up. "Because the naughty ladies liked to play Post Office?"

She laughed. "No, because the post office is on this street. A couple of blocks down that way." She pointed to her right. "Some of the bawdy houses were quite grand, I understand, and they operated quite openly from the late eighteen-hundreds until they were closed down in the fifties."

"Where were the police all this time?"

"Taking bribes, I imagine," Tess answered as they walked on. "Or simply looking the other way. Underneath its genteel facade, Galveston was a wild and wooly, wide-open town. Even during Prohibition and in the later days when most of Texas was dry, liquor flowed freely here, and there were lots of gambling clubs on the island that made a few of its residents rich. You should hear Aunt Olivia tell about the Texas Rangers throwing slot machines into the Gulf and raiding some of the fancier gaming rooms. She was incensed that the Texas attorney general butted into the island's business. Most people around here simply winked and ignored the town's vices and eccentricities. They still do. Galvestonians are a tolerant lot."

"Do you mean it's still going on?"

Tess straightened her spine and feigned a wide-eyed look. "Why, Mista Friday," she drawled, "such things are illegal in Texas."

They both laughed and, as they continued their walk, she slipped her hand into his as if it were the most natural thing in the world. His fingers closed around hers and, as Dan looked at her, his eyes shone with indulgent tenderness and an unspoken promise of things to come. It was a potent look, and Tess felt almost giddy from it.

A few minutes later, they arrived at Sea Song Gallery, which was on the Strand, two doors down from the Mermaid. Tess introduced Dan to Nancy Vaughn, a slender black woman who was her partner in the gallery. When a customer came in, Tess wiggled her fingers at Nancy and led Dan back to the storeroom.

"These are the ones we have to hang," she said, pointing out a dozen large paintings and a half dozen smaller ones, still in their wrappings from the framer. "Let's do the big ones first."

She and Dan worked well together. In half an hour they had stripped off all the coverings and had tentatively placed the larger oils along the walls and display flats. Tess went back to the storeroom for a pair of the smaller watercolor pieces, and when she returned, she found Dan sitting on the floor, staring at one of the canvases that leaned against a cream-colored wall.

"Dan?" He didn't look up. She knelt beside him and touched his shoulder. "Dan, is something wrong?"

As if in a fog, he turned to her. "Pardon?"

"I asked if something was wrong."

He shook his head and turned back to the painting, a three-by-five foot underwater fantasy of cavorting sea nymphs. "This is magnificent. They're all magnificent." He waved his hand over the collection. "I've never seen such an unusual combination of power and delicacy. I can almost hear the musical sounds of the ocean and the nymphs' laughter."

Tess grinned as Dan rose and went from one to the other, studying each of the paintings, about half of which were abstracts. "Good. You're supposed to be able to. It's called the Sea Song series in honor of the formal opening of the gallery."

"This is a local artist?" Dan sounded surprised. "Tess, every one of these paintings is museum-quality." He peered at the lower right corner of two of the pieces. "Who is it? The only signature I can make out is something that looks like a fishhook."

"It *is* a fishhook," she said. "That's the way he signs all his work."

"So it is a man. I couldn't be sure. Something in the style and power of the strokes told me it was, but I couldn't imagine the same man being able to express such delicacy and sensitivity." He went back to sit beside Tess in front of the underwater fantasy. "This one particularly fascinates me. Something about the nymphs seems familiar."

"Picture me nude."

A devilish gleam came in his eye. "I have. Many times."

She gave him a playful swat on the shoulder. "Nude with great swirls of blue hair longer than I am."

Dan looked from Tess to the painting and back again. "My God, it's you!" She grinned and his eyes narrowed and his nostrils flared as a rush of irrational fury flashed through him. The thought of anyone, even an artist, seeing his Tess nude angered him. *He* hadn't even seen her nude yet. "Did you pose for this?" His words were sharp.

Her eyes widened. "Are you such a prude?" She sounded amused.

"Did you?" There was no humor in his question.

"Only the face is mine. The rest is pure imagination."

Dan felt his gut relax.

Tess rose and tugged at Dan's hand. "Come on. I want to show you something." She led him to a painting with another female fantasy figure and hoisted the large oil to eye level. "Look closely at the face of this one."

He squinted and leaned toward the stylized mermaid with copper hair.

"Look familiar?"

He glanced at Tess and frowned. "It reminds me of your Aunt Olivia."

Tess smiled. "And that one?" She pointed to another leaning against a flat.

Dan squatted and looked at the central figure whose flowing white hair was studded with starfish. "Gram?"

She nodded again. "Your grandmother was delighted to be immortalized as a sea siren. Hook got a kick out of it, too."

"Hook?" Dan glanced at the corner of the painting, then up at Tess. "Do you mean . . . Hook?" He sketched the big man's distinctive scar on his own face, tapped his front tooth, and pointed to large oil. "*Hook* painted this?"

Looking smug, Tess slowly nodded her head.

"My God," Dan whispered, stunned. "He's an ex-con."

"A sensitive, very talented ex-con. My grandmother and Aunt Olivia first saw his work in a Huntsville Prison art show."

"I can't believe it. Tess, I promise you, these paintings are fabulous."

"I know. Several have bought his work."

"And he stays on as your aunt's houseman?"

While they hung Hook's paintings, Tess told him the story of how her grandmother and her aunt had hired an attorney and used their considerable influence to secure Hook's parole in their custody.

"It helps when you know the governor personally," she said as they placed the last of the watercolors. "They recognized Hook's potential, and he was grateful for their faith in him. He's completely devoted to Aunt Olivia, as he was to my grandmother before she died. Hook says they gave him a chance when nobody else would. They outfitted a studio in his apartment over the garage and saw that he had art lessons and all the supplies he needed."

"It's amazing. I still can't comprehend that somebody who looks like Hook can paint pictures that look like this."

"Believe it." She cocked her head and gave him a complacent grin. "Are you feeling a bit sheepish about judging him by his looks?" When he nodded, looking appropriately contrite, she said, "Good. You're learning. Come on, let's get the rest of these up."

By the time they were finished, it was dark outside and Nancy had gone home. With Dan's arm draped casually around her shoulders, they stood surveying their work.

"I think we did a fine job," he said. "We make a good team."

"A darned good team," Tess agreed, slipping her arm around his lean waist.

"I can't remember when I've enjoyed an afternoon more. I hate for it to end."

"It was fun, wasn't it?" She glanced at her watch. "It's almost dinnertime. We'd better get home or

Ivan will have our hide. You've become his personal project, you know."

"Why don't we have dinner out for a change? Think Ivan would mind if we gave him a call?"

Tess shook her head.

After they phoned, Tess locked the gallery and they walked toward the waterfront. With the loss of the sun, the night air was crisp and chilly. They walked snuggled close together, arms wrapped around each other's waists and laughing as they bumped hips until they matched the tempo of their strides.

Although she'd been happy living in Galveston for some time now, Tess had never felt more profoundly alive than she did at that moment. Hers. Daniel Friday was hers. A thrill of joy rippled over her and she shivered.

"You're cold," Dan said, running his hands over the goose bumps on her arms. "And I don't have a jacket to offer you."

"I'm fine."

Spotting a souvenir shop that was still open, Dan pulled her inside and insisted on buying her something warm. "Though I hate to cover up that lion's eye. He's been winking at me all afternoon."

They laughed over the funny sayings printed on some of the shirts and clowned around holding some of the more outrageous ones to their shoulders to model. A few minutes later they left, attired in matching hot pink sweatshirts with cross-eyed green frogs and *LIFE'S A BEACH* stamped across the front.

"It's *you*," Tess said, standing back to admire his gaudy choice and crossing her eyes to mimic the frog.

Dan threw back his head and laughed. Scooping her up into his arm, he hugged her close. "Tess

Cameron, you do strange things to my conservative sensibilities."

"Good." She tucked her hand under the band of his sweatshirt and let it rest on the warmth of his belly. "Your conservative sensibilities need a little shaking up. They've given you nothing but trouble."

Since their confrontation at noon, Dan's behavior had made a hundred and eighty-degree turn—well, maybe closer to a hundred degrees—and Tess was keeping her fingers crossed that he wouldn't revert to the foul-tempered, straitlaced stinker she knew he could be. She liked him much better the way he was now. She suspected that she was beginning to see the real Dan, who'd been hiding away inside a carefully constructed shell. Even if he'd rather die than admit it, she was sure that Kathy and the board had been right to toss him out. Only his damnable male pride had been injured.

The more she was around Dan, the clearer it became that he hated being an executive at Friday Elevators, and he probably always had. How awful that his sense of responsibility to his family had made him endure it for years. No wonder his misery had finally eaten a hole in his stomach; he had the soul of an architect. Anybody with half a brain could see that.

If she had anything to do with it, Tess planned to help Dan follow his own dreams for a change.

With Tess pointing the way, they crossed the intersection and walked a block to Water Street, toward a two-story wooden structure extending over the dark water. From a half a block away, delicious aromas of cooking seafood filled the air, overpowering the odors from the wharf and its shrimp boats and fish markets. Her mouth watered.

"Doesn't it smell wonderful?" Tess asked as they stepped into the smoky restaurant, where a battalion of cooks and servers scampered back and forth behind the cafeteria-type counter in a flurry of activity. "I'm starved. What looks good to you?"

Dan studied the menu painted on a huge wooden sign at the beginning of the line. "I want a giant platter of fried shrimp, french fries, and about a quart of catsup."

Tess drew her brows together in reproach. "Nothing fried for you, my friend. Say, do you have your medication?"

"In my pocket," Dan grumbled.

"*I'll* order," Tess informed him as they picked up trays and slid them along the rail. "Two broiled snapper and two baked potatoes," she told the attendant. "Plain rolls—no garlic butter."

"Not even a small order of french fries?" Dan asked wistfully.

Tess pursed her lips and shook her head slowly. "Not even one."

Dan sighed theatrically. Tess giggled.

"You may have pudding. Do you prefer banana, vanilla, or tapioca?"

"Chocolate."

"Chocolate it is." She plunked a bowl of chocolate pudding on his tray and banana on hers, then selected milk for him and iced tea for herself. When he opened his mouth to protest, she gave him her sternest look.

"Yes, Mother," he said and grinned.

They took their trays upstairs to a large, informal dining room with walls of windows overlooking the dark outlines of the shrimp and fishing boats docked at Pier 19.

"This has always been called the 'Mosquito Fleet Berth,' " Tess explained as they ate, pointing out the insectlike profiles of the small boats along the wharf. "It's the same area Jean Laffite's pirate ships used for docking."

She could have bitten her tongue off the moment the words were out of her mouth. Things had been going so well between them.

Right on cue, Dan asked casually, "What about this map you mentioned?"

Tess sighed and put her fork down. "I know it sounds bizarre unless you know the family history." She leaned closer and said in a low voice, "It's not something that's widely known, but Jean Laffite was my great-great-great-great-great—is that five?" she asked as she counted the "greats" on her fingers. "Anyway, he was my grandfather several generations back."

Dan raised a skeptical eyebrow.

"It's true!" she said, exasperated. "Our branch is descended from the daughter, and only child, of his second wife, Contessa. I'm named for her. She was a young woman from South Carolina, and she died in childbirth in 1826. Their daughter's name was Violet and she grew up on her grandparents' plantation near Charleston. She stayed with them even after Laffite married again a few years later, moved to St. Louis, and changed his name. I gather that there was some animosity between her grandparents and Laffite. When Violet married in 1843, her father gave her a deed to property in the newly formed city of Galveston and a Bible with the treasure map inside."

He continued to eat his fish as if he didn't believe a single thing she said. Refusing to look at him or to utter another word, Tess picked up her fork and attacked her own food with a vengeance.

When he had scraped the last drop of pudding from his bowl, Dan leaned back and laced his fingers across the green frog on his chest. "Tess, as a boy I was fascinated with pirates and privateers. I used to have quite a collection of books about them. As I recall, Jean Laffite died shortly after he was run off Campeche and Galveston island by the United States government. That would have been some time in the eighteen-twenties."

"Nope," she said, pushing a slice of banana to the side of her bowl, where she had deposited several others. "He died in 1854."

"Tess—"

"What?" Irritated, she looked up, ready to do battle. He was staring at her bowl.

"Why didn't you get vanilla pudding if you're not going to eat the bananas?"

"Because I *like* banana pudding. I just don't like the bananas."

Dan shook his head and gave a mirthless chuckle. "I suppose that makes as much sense as anything else you've said."

She put her spoon down and looked up at him. "You don't believe me, do you?"

He shrugged as a smile began to play around his lips. "I guess you should know if you like bananas or not."

"That's not what I mean, and you know it."

He leaned forward and took one of her hands in his. "Tess, I promised I wouldn't jump to any more conclusions without all the facts. And right now I don't want to argue with you. I can think of at least ten things I'd rather do."

His thumb brushed back and forth across her knuckles and his eyes were on her lips.

"Oh?" A slow smile came as she began to imagine what some of those things might be.

He nodded. "Let's go."

As the horse's hooves clip-clopped along the asphalt street, Tess and Dan sat snuggled close together in the old-fashioned carriage. His arms were around her and her head rested on his shoulder as they looked up at the stars and listened to the banter of the driver, an elderly gentleman in a top hat. A crisp breeze ruffled Tess's hair and a stray lock tickled Dan's nose.

He smoothed the strand back. "Comfortable?"

"Very."

"This isn't what we get when we call a taxi in Pittsburgh."

"But isn't this better? No exhaust fumes." She burrowed closer. "And much more romantic."

They were content with the quiet and one another as they rode slowly through neighborhoods of old houses and tree-lined streets. Shadows of the night kindly disguised the buildings with rotting boards and peeling paint and revealed only the dramatic lines of their former elegance.

Tess reveled in the comfort of Dan's arms around her, the warm pulsations of his strong body next to hers, the smell of him that permeated the shoulder of the soft sweatshirt where she rested her cheek.

The emotions he aroused in her were almost overwhelming, and snatches of fantasies she dared not allow full birth made her wiggle with anticipation. She thought of the things yet to come, things

that would come slowly, to be savored and trea-
sured. Not for a moment did she question that love
would grow between them. She could sense it beginning to stir and send out roots deep inside her. She
imagined the feel of his bare skin next to hers and
she snuggled closer.

"Cold?"

She shook her head. "My frog keeps me warm."

He chuckled and gave her a little squeeze.

The horse-drawn carriage pulled to a stop in the
back parking lot of a hotel that fronted the seawall.
Daniel climbed down and helped Tess descend.

"I'll get a cup of coffee across the street while you
and your young man take a walk," the driver said to
Tess.

"We won't be long, Amos. It's a bit nippy tonight."

"Take your time, li'l lady. Me and Snooks don't
have nothing better to do."

"Thanks, Amos." Tess waved at the old man, and
she and Dan crossed the boulevard.

"He's a character," Dan said as they walked down
the steps to a deserted strip of beach lit by the moon
and street lights along the seawall. "Do you own
fifty-one percent of the horse?"

Tess laughed. "No, Amos and I are just friends.
I've known him since I was a little girl and spent
every summer here with my grandmother and Aunt
Olivia. I like to ride with him once or twice a week in
the off-season when he isn't too busy."

"To make sure Snooks has enough oats?"

She shrugged.

He smiled. "That's what I thought." He took her
hand and they walked along the damp sand near the
water's edge. "Where did you spend your winters?"

"In Galveston until I was about four. My mother

died shortly after I was born, and I lived with my grandmother and Aunt Olivia until my father remarried. Then I went to live with him and my stepmother in Dallas."

"Do you have brothers or sisters?"

"Two younger half brothers. They both work in my father's bank and are very happy. They're 'chips off the old block.' We're not close. I never fit in very well with that part of the family."

They paused to watch the waves lap the beach and Dan smiled. "I'm not surprised. Somehow I can't see you as the conservative banker type."

"Oh, but I was." Tess turned to look up at Dan. "Or at least I tried to be. I have an MBA in finance and was a money manager in the trust department of Dad's bank until I was recruited by an investment firm in New York. I was sort of a whiz kid with investments."

Dan's eyebrows raised. "You?"

"Me."

"Somehow I can't picture a woman who plays the bagpipe and drives a car named Buttercup as a banker or an investment consultant."

She laughed. "Pin-striped suits, red power ties, and all. I led the rat race for several years."

"What happened?"

"Aunt Olivia broke her hip, and I came to Galveston to take care of her. Once I got off the treadmill and had some time to take a look at my life, I discovered I hated the city and my job. Funny, I never thought of it as a career, only a job. I found that I hadn't really laughed or enjoyed myself in years. Money and investments had become the prime focus of my world. I was extremely *dedicated*." Tess made a dramatic gesture, then laughed at herself.

She looked down and patted a broken shell into the sand with the tip of her shoe. "But while I was here and had time to take stock of things, something in me rebelled against living my life according to what I thought I *should* do. When time came for me to go back, I couldn't do it. And there was really no reason to. I love this island, the people, the slower pace and freedom I have here. I'd made enough money so that, properly invested, I would have enough to last me the rest of my life. So, instead of catching a plane back to New York, I called and resigned. I've never regretted it, and I've never been happier. Now I do what *I* want to do."

Dan looked out over the Gulf and was quiet for a moment. The breeze scattered the rising moon's reflection across the dark water. Only the roar of waves splashing against the jetties and tumbling over one another as they rolled into shore broke the silence. His hand gripped hers tightly, and Tess could feel his inner turmoil as she watched him. After what seemed like forever, but was only a few minutes, he turned to her.

Lifting her chin with the crook of his finger, he smiled and said, "I'm very glad you made the decision to stay in Galveston. If you were still in New York, I might never have met you."

He leaned forward and slanted his lips over hers in the gentlest of kisses. Nuzzling his cheek against the tip of her nose, Dan said, "Your nose is cold. We should go."

"Not yet," Tess said in a throaty whisper. Her arms went around his waist and she lifted her mouth to him once more.

"Lord, Tess, I ache for you." He gathered her close

and, with a low groan deep in his throat, covered her lips with his.

She clung to him as his tongue plundered the warm secrets of mouth and his strong hands kneaded the curves of her back. One arm slipped down to scoop her pelvis closer against him, and Tess whimpered. Waves of warmth, more powerful than the ocean's, dashed over her and drove away the chill of wind and water.

Time and place were swept away in the ebb and flow of delicious sensation. Fingers clutched and stroked; bodies pressed and arched; lips and tongues explored and tasted and murmured their pleasure.

"Tess?" Dan said as he nipped and nuzzled along the soft curve of her neck.

Her knees were like limp rubber bands and she could barely manage a breathless "Yes?"

"I think my feet are wet."

Tess looked down at the tide lapping against their ankles and her shoulders began to shake.

Five

Dressed in electric blue silk harem pants and flowing tunic top, Tess stood in front of the painting and sipped from her champagne glass. Her earrings, long falls of gold-dipped shells mixed with fiery blue beads and hammered gold disks, matched the elaborate necklace that hung to her waist and tinkled like wind chimes each time she moved. Across her forehead she wore a headband of blue silk braided with the same beads that accented her jewelry and on her feet she wore strapped sandals.

She'd fussed endlessly with her clothes and hair and makeup, wanting to look just right for the formal opening of Sea Song—and for Dan, she admitted frankly. Strangely enough, she'd been nervous when she walked down the stairs to meet him earlier. Her efforts had been rewarded when Dan, looking like a million dollars in his dark suit and the new pink shirt and mauve paisley tie she'd insisted he buy, had raised one eyebrow and whistled.

She'd looked him up and down and whistled back.

He moved to her side now. "Somebody's already bought the cavorting nymphs I see," she said, pointing to the "Sold" tag.

"Ummm." Dan took a swallow of water from his crystal stem. "Somebody." He slipped his arm around her waist and the heel of his palm caressed the swell of her hip with tiny strokes.

The feigned innocence in his tone made her look back at him. "Would you happen to be the somebody?"

He grinned. "I couldn't let some bozo buy it so he could sit and drool over your face and fantasize about blue-haired sea nymphs nibbling his toes."

Tess widened her eyes and pursed her lips to fight back a giggle. "Nibbling his toes?"

He shrugged and his grin widened devilishly. "It's *my* fantasy." His hand slipped a little lower.

As his hand slid along the outer curve of her hip, she almost came unglued. "Daniel," she whispered, scolding. "There is a room full of people here."

He sighed and moved his hand. She giggled over the rim of her champagne glass.

"Did you buy the one of your grandmother too?"

Daniel shook his head and gave her a look that almost fused her beads. He leaned over and whispered, "My grandmother doesn't turn me on."

"Oh, there you two are!" Martha Craven bustled over, smiling, and with her hands clasped beneath her chin. "Isn't this a grand affair? I want you to come meet a lovely couple here from Dallas, the Turners. They bought the painting of me." Whispering, she added, "The one of Olivia hasn't sold yet, and I think she's a little miffed."

Martha steered Dan and Tess back into the mainstream of the party. They met the Turners, then they listened to the harpist who sat in a corner amid the potted ferns and ficus trees. Later they sampled the buffet, presided over by an ebullient Ivan in a green polka-dot ascot and Olivia in a silk caftan painted with the markings of a monarch butterfly. They met and mixed and smiled until after midnight, when the last of the many guests and patrons left the gallery.

"Tired?" Dan asked as he drove Buttercup home.

She nodded and leaned her head back against the seat. "But it's a good tired. Didn't Hook look smashing in his red silk pirate's shirt? I'm so happy for him. Every one of his paintings sold."

"The gallery made a nice commission too."

"Yes, I'm so pleased for Nancy."

"Your partner?"

Tess nodded. "She can use the extra money. She's divorced and has three small children to support."

"How did you two get together?"

"I met her when I was doing some volunteer work for the battered women's shelter. Oh, Dan, if you could have seen her then, it almost broke my heart. She was so cowed and dispirited. It was awful. Now she hardly looks or acts like the person I met a few months ago."

When they pulled into the drive and stopped, Daniel reached for her hand. "So you brought Nancy and the three kids home with you?"

"Only until we organized the gallery and she could find a place of her own. She's almost finished her degree in art history, you know. She's a very bright lady."

"Gram told me you found Luis living in a box in an alley behind the Strand. I'll bet you were the kind of little girl who brought home stray kittens and puppies."

Tess laughed and snuggled close to his side. "I tried, but it didn't work out very well. I'm allergic to cats and dogs."

Dan was quiet for a moment. Then he lifted her chin and very gently kissed her. "Am I one of your strays, Tess?"

She only laughed again at his teasing and lifted her face to his.

It was a glorious sunshiny morning—a perfect beach day. Dan deposited Tess's bagpipe into the back of a miniature pedal-driven surrey covered with a red and white striped canopy.

"Are you sure you wouldn't rather rent some roller skates?" Tossing one long end of her fringed, tie-dyed scarf over her shoulder aviator-style, she hitched up the legs of her screaming yellow jumpsuit and climbed in.

"Not me. Olivia told me that's the way she broke her hip." He grinned as they headed down the side of the boulevard. "Pedal, woman, or I'm going to get a hernia."

Tess laughed and started pedaling.

Tess and Dan had spent almost every moment of the past several days together. They had toured historic homes and museums, visited Sea-Arama and watched the dolphins and sharks. They had ridden the carousel and the Ferris wheel at Stewart Beach and had played Monopoly and Scrabble, and in the evening they had gone to a couple of old movies at the Opera House. Unfortunately, most of the time they hadn't been alone. And Tess decided it was tough to start a romance when four chaperones watched their every move.

Today was different. It was theirs. Aunt Martha and Aunt Olivia were tied up with their monthly, all-day Kaffeeklatsch; Hook was working in his studio; and Ivan was giving a workshop in French sauces in Houston.

Each day, it seemed to Tess, another of Dan's frown lines disappeared. He was laughing more, relaxing more. Only rarely did she catch a glimpse of the obsessive sobersides she'd met that day on the pier. She was certain that a month ago he wouldn't have been caught dead in the cornflower blue sweatsuit he was wearing now. He was growing tan and faint sun-streaks highlighted his hair. Although it hardly seemed possible, he had become more handsome. And more desirable. Her toes curled just looking at him.

"Wake up, woman, and start pedaling. I'm doing all the work."

Tess laughed again and resumed pumping.

After they lunched at one of the seafood restaurants that faced the Gulf, they decided it was warm enough for sunbathing and went to the car to fetch towels and lotion.

They found a secluded stretch of beach, deserted except for a few sandpipers scampering back and forth as the waves gently teased and retreated along the shore.

"This looks like a good spot," Tess said, giving her towel a snap to spread it on the warm sand. "We'll probably have it all to ourselves. The weather's too temperamental for the tourists at this time of year. One day it's cool or drizzly and the next it's hot as Hades."

Dan spread his towel beside hers, kicked off his shoes, and shucked his shirt and pants. Tess tried not to stare. She really did. She meant to be blasé and super-cool. But she's never seen him without a shirt, without pants. Her mouth went dry, and her knees started doing their rubber band number again.

He was dynamite. The bathing suit, an abbreviated boxer in light blue, hung low on his lean hips and stretched over well-muscled thighs dusted with sandy colored hair. His shoulders were broad and a patch of light brown curls lay across pectorals that told her Daniel Friday hadn't spent all his time behind a desk.

She gaped at him. When she managed to drag her gaze from the corded plane of his abdomen to his face, his eyes were crinkled with laughter and a smile played at the edges of his mouth.

"Like what you see?" he asked.

"Is the pope Catholic?"

He threw back his head and laughed. "Tess Cameron, there's nothing coy about you."

She cocked her head and frowned. "Does my lack of subtlety bother you, Dan?"

He shook his head, very slowly. "The only thing bothering me now is the waiting."

"The waiting?"

He nodded and the right corner of his mouth made a slow ascent. "It's my turn to play voyeur." Standing with feet apart, hands resting on his hips, he gave her a look that could have melted her zipper.

And that must have been what happened.

In her imagination, she pictured herself drawing the zipper of her jumpsuit down in a fluid, tantalizing motion. With one shrug of her shoulders, the fabric would slide slowly down her body and pool at her feet. She would gracefully step out of it, smile seductively, arch her back, and he would be struck dumb with the wonder of her scantily clad body.

The zipper stuck.

She tugged and yanked, but the little sucker only chewed further into the material. "Damn!" she muttered, yanking harder.

"Here, let me try it." Dan moved her sweaty hands, patiently worked the fabric free, and slid the zipper down. "There." He stepped back and resumed his pose.

Mortified, Tess managed something she hoped resembled a smile and shrugged her shoulders. The jumpsuit slid only as far as her elbows and trapped her like a straitjacket.

If he laughs at me, I'll kill him.

Sober-faced—though his tight lips twitched suspiciously—Dan watched every awkward contortion, until she finally managed to free her arms. The garment slipped to her ankles revealing a silvered, pale pink suit with high-cut legs, very little back, and no middle at all.

Dan's eyes widened, and she heard him suck in a breath. Tess smiled seductively, arched slightly, and took a step forward.

If Dan hadn't grabbed her, she'd have plunked nose down in the sand.

She'd forgotten to take off her sneakers.

"Oh, God, I could die," she groaned as she hopped around on one foot, then the other, trying to pull the tight pants legs over her shoes. She stopped her hopping to glare at Dan. "And if you laugh at me, Daniel Friday, I'll emasculate you with a rusty knife."

A series of strangling sounds came from Dan's throat, but he didn't crack a smile. "Sit down, honey, and let me untie your shoes."

She couldn't even do that gracefully. The jumpsuit wrapped around her ankles like shackles swished back and forth in the sand as she took shuffling baby steps to the towel. She bent her knees and rocked back on her bottom with a thump. Falling to her back, she looked up at the clear blue sky and wished for a giant tidal wave to crash over her and wash her off the face of the earth.

Dan knelt, put her feet across his thighs, and began to untie her shoes.

"Oh, Lord," she groaned.

"What's the matter, honey?"

"Need you ask? I'm humiliated out of my mind." Tess flung her arm over her eyes. "I'm always such a klutz when I get nervous. Instead of looking glamorous and sexy, I was flopping around like a wounded chicken."

Dan tossed her shoes aside and his hand slipped along the outer curve of her calf. He laughed softly. "I've never seen a chicken with legs like these." His hand slid upward to her thigh, then down toward her ankle again. "So long and beautiful. And very, very sexy."

Dan's gaze swept over the length of her from red toenails to lush dark hair. Nothing about her sweetly curved body escaped his attention, and he felt himself becoming aroused. Lord, if Tess only knew what she did to him. He'd been attracted to her from the moment he'd first seen her on the pier, and every day the lure of her grew stronger. Never had he wanted any woman the way he wanted Tess. Everything about her enchanted him, delighted him, stirred a deep hunger in an empty spot somewhere inside him.

"Do you really think so?" she said. "It's hard to

think of myself as sexy. I looked like an undernourished flamingo until I was seventeen. I towered over everybody and was always stumbling over my own feet." She wiggled her toes.

Before today, he'd never seen the vulnerable side of Tess. In fact, he'd have bet anyone that she was never ruffled by anything or had a single self-doubt. Her nervousness and awkwardness in getting out of her clothes had only made her more endearing. And it made keeping himself in check even more difficult. He was obsessed with her.

Taking a deep, fortifying breath, Dan pulled the bright yellow jumpsuit over her feet and laid the garment beside the sneakers. "You're beautiful, Tess. And sexy. Surely you've been told that before."

His fingers ached to wander over her soft skin and explore every golden dip and plane. He could imagine the silken texture of her belly and her breasts. Almost of its own accord, his hand came up and reached toward her. Cursing himself for his own weakness, he snatched it back and curled his fingers into a fist to resist the urge.

For his own sanity, he'd been trying to convince himself that he could limit their relationship to a friendship or a casual flirtation. Now he realized such a notion was a dangerous delusion. He was very close to falling in love with Tess, and allowing himself to touch her the way he wanted to would be inviting emotional disaster. He knew he was only an object of her enormous compassion. And it humiliated him. He would not be another downtrodden soul Tess had dragged home to tend.

Gently, he moved her feet from his thighs, stretched out prone on his towel, and turned his face from her.

Tess raised herself up on her elbows and frowned at the back of Dan's head. She didn't understand his behavior. She didn't understand it at all.

"Dan?" His reply was a half-grunt. "Is there someone back in Pittsburgh?"

"There are lots of people in Pittsburgh."

She sighed. He wasn't going to make it easy. "I mean is there someone special . . . a woman . . . someone you . . ."

"No," he said quietly. "There's no one."

"And you find me attractive?"

"Yes."

"Then why are you acting so peculiar?"

"I don't know what you're talking about."

Tess rolled her eyes heavenward in a silent entreaty. "I could carry on a more enlightening conversation with a pelican." She rummaged through her bag and pulled out a bottle of sunscreen. When she drizzled a long streak down Dan's back, he jerked. When she straddled his hips, he jerked again.

"What are you doing?" His tone was short.

"I'm putting lotion on you so that you won't blister," she said in her most patient voice. Using both hands, she began to spread the thick liquid over his back. "I thought you were learning to relax. You're as tight as a tick."

Loving the feel of him under her hands, she smiled and ran her thumbs along the edge of his spine. He tensed even more. The muscles of his neck and shoulders were as knotted and lumpy as flophouse pillows. His legs, she noticed as she moved to apply lotion to them, weren't any better. She kneaded and massaged, but the muscles bunched tighter.

"Want me to do your front?" she asked.

"Later."

"Would you please put some on me?"

He gave a muffled grunt.

"Is that a yes or a no?"

"Tess, please," he groaned.

"Please what? What in the hell is wrong with you, Daniel Friday? Are you ill? Is your stomach bothering you?"

"No."

"Then it must be me. Am I bothering you? Is the thought of my touching you or your touching me so repulsive?" She snatched up her jumpsuit. "Well, fine! Just fine! You can—"

Dan rose to his knees and gripped her upper arms. "Your touch repulsive?" His fingers tightened and his eyes burned. "My Lord, woman, are you crazy? I lie in bed every night and stare at that damned picture of the nymphs with blue hair and your face. I fantasize about your touch until I'm almost out of my mind. Then I go to sleep and dream about you. Touching you repulsive?" A mirthless laugh escaped his lips. "Being with you every day and not touching you is agony. I ache from wanting to touch you. Right now I'd like to—"

He closed his eyes and, teeth clenched together so hard the muscles in his jaw quivered, sucked in a deep shuddering gulp of air.

"What would you like to do, Dan?" Her question was a husky whisper.

He opened his eyes and their gazes locked. In his eyes she saw desire, raw and burning. She saw a hunger that lit a fire in the deepest recesses of her being; she saw the pain of the man she loved. Yes, he was hers, and at that moment she loved him with a fierceness that defied reason. She would have waded through broken glass and fought tigers to get to him.

"What would you like to do?" she whispered again. "Tell me."

"I'd like to touch every incredible inch of your beautiful body. I'd like to touch you with my fingers and lick you with my tongue and taste you with my mouth. I'd like to kiss you so hard that your flesh would melt into mine. But most of all, I'd like to rip off that little pink scrap of nothing you're wearing and plunge into you so hot and deep that you would scream my name so loudly it could be heard in the next state."

She smiled a slow, languid smile. "Then why don't you?"

He gave her a little shake. "Damn you, Tess Cameron. Damn your siren's smile. And damn your beautiful eyes. Damn your sexy voice and sexy body. Damn your laughing, loving spirit. And damn me for a fool who wants it all." He almost flung her away. Sinking back on his heels, he gripped each of his knees with splayed, white-knuckled fingers and dropped his gaze.

Her smile faded. "I don't understand. Do you hate me so much?"

His eyes shot up. "Hate you?" His laugh had a hollow ring. "I don't hate you, Tess. Far from it. How could I hate the saint of Galveston? Give Mother Teresa a gorgeous body, a slightly crazy family, and a set of bagpipes, and the two of you could pass for twins."

Tess frowned. "Dan, what are you talking about? I'm no saint."

"You're not? Hook told me that Becky was an unwed mother on welfare until you helped her open the Mermaid. He also said that one of your boutiques is managed by a good-looking Vietnam veteran named Hank who's a recovering alcoholic and the other by a woman who's a paraplegic. And then there's Nancy at the gallery, and Luis."

"So? They're all very competent people." She searched his face, trying to fathom his line of reasoning. "You're not making a lick of sense. How is all that related to your touching me?"

Shifting his position so that he lay on one hip and was propped up by his elbow, he scooped up a handful of sand and watched it slowly sift through his fingers.

"My self-respect has taken enough of a beating in the past few weeks. You've helped me through a rough time, and I sincerely appreciate it. But I don't want to be just another stray you've brought home. Tess, leave me with some pride."

As the light slowly dawned, Tess had the strangest urge to strangle him.

"So you think I consider you a humanitarian project in need of a little tea and sympathy?" she asked.

He looked pained.

"I see." She stretched out beside Dan, reclining on her elbow, mirroring his pose. With one finger she traced a lazy pattern through the curls of hair on his chest, and his pectorals flexed when she circled a nipple with her fingernail.

Her finger trailed up his throat, over his chin, and to the little freckle at the corner of his mouth. "It might interest you to know," she said in her most seductive tone, "that I've never had any desire to nibble Luis's toes." She ran her finger back and forth along the crease of his lips, nudging them until they parted and she touched the tip of his tongue. "I've never conjured up an image of Hank's kissing me." She leaned over and dropped a feather-light peck on his lower lip. "And I've never"—she circled his mouth with the tip of her tongue as her foot slid up his leg—"never fallen in love with a single one of them."

Dan groaned. "Tess . . ."

She laughed a low, husky invitation. "Friday, you're such an idiot."

His arms went around her, and he rolled her onto her back. His mouth covered hers with a low growl, and his tongue thrust between her lips. Tess held him close, feeling as if she were drowning in sensation. His hand stroked upward over the curve of her hip, her rib cage, and his palm paused at the outer swell of her breast. She strained toward it.

Dan was sure he was in heaven as he trailed his tongue along the soft hollow of her throat, tasting her sweet skin. The heady fragrance of her coiled around his brain and left him mindless. To hell with self-respect. He couldn't have resisted her now for a truckload of it.

Something whacked him in the back and he grunted. "What the—"

He raised himself up and looked directly into the big brown eyes of a little girl squatting beside him. About four or five years old, she was dressed in a ruffled green sunsuit and holding a big rubber ball. Behind her were two other children and a dog.

"Hi, mister. Whatcha doin'?"

Dan growled and the mutt behind the child growled back.

Tess shook with silent laughter.

"It's not funny," Dan muttered as he looked down at her. "I can't believe you have me so crazy that I was about to make love to you on a public beach in broad daylight."

"You wanna play ball with us?" the little girl asked.

"No, thank you." Dan tried to smile.

Tess exploded with laughter.

"Wait till I get you home," Dan said. "You have some explaining to do."

Six

Tess didn't want to explain. She hadn't meant to tell Dan that she was in love with him. It was far too soon for such declarations, and she didn't want to scare him off. But neither did she want him to believe that he was no more to her than some new altruistic endeavor. Since she didn't want to discuss either issue, she chattered all the way home, not allowing him to question her.

She gave a running commentary of the history of every house and building they passed. What she didn't know, she made up. She suspected that he was on to her game for once or twice he raised his eyebrow and gave her an odd look.

"The reason Galveston has so many oleanders is an interesting story," she said as they got out of Buttercup and walked to the front porch. "There was a sea captain—or maybe he was a merchant—and I forget his name, but he brought some cuttings to his sister who lived on the island. It was about—"

"Tess."

"Yes, Dan?"

"It won't work."

She affected a look of wide-eyed innocence as she opened the front door. "What won't work?"

"Sooner or later you're bound to run down. Then we'll talk."

She received a temporary reprieve when a "yoo-hoo" rang out from the dining room. Martha Craven, her white curls scraped back from her face with a strip of cotton, poked her head around the door.

"I thought I heard you two." The older woman beckoned them. "Come in and say hello to the girls. I've told them all about my handsome grandson and they're just dying to meet you, Danny." Martha bustled toward Dan, hooked her arm through his, and propelled him along with her. "We're having a Mary Kay party—that's makeup you know—and we're almost finished."

Grinning, Tess trailed along behind the pair. Her grin widened when they entered the dining room. The five elderly ladies sitting around the table immediately snatched off their cotton headbands and began fluffing their hair and preening for the newly arrived male. It didn't matter that he was forty or fifty years younger than everyone except the middle-aged blond who was the beauty consultant.

Dan was gallant as he was introduced to the women, complimenting each of the wrinkled ladies as if she were a beauty queen. Tess felt her admiration for him grow as she watched him. He could be such a sweetheart.

One blue-haired matron examined herself in a hand mirror. "I'm trying to decide on a lipstick. Do you think this shade is flattering, Mr. Friday?"

Olivia leaned forward. "Mary Ella Hartman, you

know very well it doesn't make a dime's worth of difference which one you pick."

"Oh, I know it Olivia. I think that's the worse thing about being old. You wake up one morning and find you don't have any lips left."

"What did she say?" Lela Spillman asked Olivia.

"You need a hearing aid, Lela. You're getting as deaf as a doorpost," Olivia said loudly.

"That shade of lipstick reminds me of the color you wore in the beauty contest, Mary Ella," Irene Reynolds interrupted. "It was the same year they tore down the old Tremont Hotel—or was it the year before?" Irene Reynolds raised her eyebrows and peered over her glasses. "When your daddy saw you in that bathing costume, he marched you home and locked you in your room for three months."

The group of childhood friends launched into spirited reminiscences, and Tess and Dan winked at each other. Both were trying to suppress grins. It was obvious how much the ladies were enjoying themselves and how much such activities kept their spirits alive. Tess was sure that Dan, after spending over three weeks in Galveston, could see how happy his grandmother was and how groundless his concerns had been. Living with Aunt Olivia had brought a new sparkle to Martha Craven's face and new energy to her step.

Still smiling with indulgent amusement, Dan motioned with his head toward the exit. As they turned to sneak away, Olivia called out.

"Tess, I think that letter you've been waiting for came today."

"The one from Dr. Staats at Stanford?"

"It's on the hall table."

Her heart pounding, Tess hurried to the hallway

and snatched up the letter. She ripped it open and quickly scanned the contents. "Yippee!" she screamed, throwing both arms in the air. She grabbed Dan in a bear hug and started dancing around.

"Good news, I take it?" Dan said, unable to keep from smiling as Tess laughed and planted kisses all over his face.

Olivia and Martha scurried in from the dining room, with the beauty consultant and other ladies close on their heels.

"Is everything all right, dear?" Olivia asked.

"Everything is fabulous! Dr. Staats confirmed it."

"Oh, wonderful!" Martha Craven clapped her hands together and laughed. "Now Tess can have her house and we can—"

Olivia poked Martha in the ribs and rolled her eyes to the ladies who all had their ears tuned for a new topic of gossip. She winked at Tess and turned to the waiting women. "Come along, girls. We need to make out our order blanks." She began shooing them back to the dining room.

"But, Olivia, what in the world is going on?"

"Nothing for you to worry about, Mary Ella. Tess just had some good news from an investment, that's all. She's always been the excitable type you know. I think you should order the pink lipstick and the lipliner. It's totally awesome. Don't you agree, Martha?"

When the women were gone, Dan said, "Why do I suspect that your letter has nothing to do with an investment?"

Tess looked at the crumpled paper in her hand, then back up at Dan and laughed. "Because you're remarkably astute?"

"Well?" After a long pause, he said, "Are you going to tell me or not?"

She gave him a sassy grin and a little bob of her head. "Or not."

His eyes narrowed. "This wouldn't have anything to do with that buried treasure nonsense, would it?"

Tess dress herself up to her full five-feet nine-and-one-quarter inches and tilted her nose in the air. "It's *not* nonsense." She waved the letter in his face. "*This* proves it. Dr. Lawrence Staats is a professor at Stanford University and the country's leading handwriting expert. Authenticating historical documents is his specialty."

Realizing that she was talking loudly enough to be overheard, she lowered her voice. "I sent him a sample of handwriting from the map and letter we found, along with a small corner of the paper it's written on. He compared it to other documented samples in his possession, and he thinks that it's authentic. Our map *was* written by Jean Laffite."

When he looked skeptical, she thrust the letter at him. "Here, read it yourself if you don't believe me."

Dan read the single page quickly. "I notice that he leaves himself an out. He writes that the paper is 'consistent with samples manufactured in the early-to mid-eighteen hundreds' and based on his preliminary study, there is 'strong indication' that the handwriting sample you sent matches other documents known to have been written by Laffite."

"Friday, you're such a hard-nose." She grabbed him by the hand. "Come upstairs with me."

When they entered the second-floor sitting room that Olivia and Martha shared, Tess sat him down in an easy chair and went to a large trunk in the corner. She took several items from the humpbacked chest, which smelled of camphor and age, and settled herself on the ottoman at Dan's feet.

"Here is the Bible Laffite gave to his daughter Violet." She opened a wooden case that was about ten by twelve inches. Inside the worn, velvet lining was a remarkably well-preserved Bible. She opened it carefully. "This is the date of Violet's wedding. And here are the names of her parents."

"But it says her father was named Theodore Lucas."

"I'll explain that later. Look at all these dates that are recorded." She pointed out the birth of twin daughters, Electra and Amelia, born to Violet the year after her wedding. Also listed were various births and deaths and marriages of the generations up to the birth of Tess's mother Anna in 1934, the death of Anna's father in World War II, and Anna's marriage to Robert Thomas Cameron.

"Aunt Olivia told me her grandmother Casey Prophet, the one who was married to the Texas Ranger, died about two years before I was born. She must have recorded the last entries, and then the Bible was packed away with her things."

"I still don't understand what this has to do with the pirate."

"Privateer," Tess corrected. "Be patient and I'll show you. Notice the front of the Bible case."

Dan closed the wooden box and looked at the crazed surface with seven multicolored stones embedded in a meandering rainbow trail. "What am I supposed to see?"

"I'm coming to that." She handed him two sheets of yellowed, worn paper encased in plastic. A corner of one—the sample she'd sent to Dr. Staats—was missing. "This is the letter that was in the Bible."

Dan looked exasperated. "It's in *French*."

"I know that! Laffite was French."

"What does it say? In English, please."

Tess laughed. "In essence, it's written to 'My darling daughter' and says that he had left her because he had many enemies intent on doing him harm. Her mother's family had told Violet that Theodore Lucas, her father, was dead, because they didn't approve of his privateering. Although he assures her that it was an honorable endeavor and he always secured the appropriate letters of marque. He says that he had thought of Violet often and that now on the occasion of her marriage, he wanted her to have this Bible, that would provide for the spiritual and *material* benefit of herself, her children, and her children's children. Each time she looked at the stones on the case she was to remember the wealth of love that her father felt for her."

Dan frowned. "It's a very nice story, Tess. But I haven't heard anything that convinces me her father was really Jean Laffite. During that period there were lots of privateers."

Tess handed him a photocopied sheet of paper. "This is a page from a translation of Laffite's memoirs which were written between 1845 and 1850. The original journal, in French, is in a museum near here. Don't raise your eyebrows at me, Daniel Friday. I'll admit that there is some controversy about its authenticity, but several prominent historians, including Dr. Staats, believe that it's genuine. Notice the highlighted area. He says that he gave his name as *Theodore Lucas* to some English captain. It was one of the many aliases Laffite used." She smiled smugly.

"Does the journal mention Violet or Contessa?"

Her face fell. "Well, no. But I'm sure there's some plausible explanation."

He took her hand and brought it to his lips. His

eyes were gentle and his expression tender. "Honey, I'll admit there are some strong coincidences, but don't pin your hopes on something so flimsy. I don't want you to be hurt."

Tess should have felt warmed by his concern, but she didn't. His condescending attitude irritated her to no end. "Give me credit for *some* brains!" She snatched her hand away. "I never realized just how stubborn you are, Friday. When you make up your mind about something, an act of Congress wouldn't change it."

"Are you insinuating that I'm closed-minded?"

"I'm not insinuating anything. I'm telling you flat out. You're closed-minded. You haven't even heard all the evidence and already you've decided that I'm suffering from some sort of nutty delusion. What is it with you? I thought you were getting over your stick-in-the-mud attitudes, but they've just been lurking in a dark corner waiting to reappear, haven't they? You're quick to claim that you don't jump to conclusions, but let me tell you, up until now I haven't seen any evidence that would convince me of it."

Dan started to say something, then paused and took a breath. "I'm sorry, Tess. Perhaps you're right. I know this is important to you. Why don't you show me the rest of the things?"

"No!"

"Now who's being stubborn?"

Tess shot to her feet and planted her hands on her hips. Her eyes narrowed. "I don't have to prove anything to you. None of this is any of your business anyway."

"Children, children," Olivia said as she came into the room with Martha close on her heels. "What's going on? We could hear you all the way downstairs."

"Your grandson," Tess said to Martha, "is undoubtedly the most pig-headed man I've ever met!"

Martha cocked her head. "Danny always has been a wee bit stubborn."

"Gram!"

Tess crossed her arms and gave Dan a smug, I-told-you-so look. "*He* doesn't believe that we know where Laffite's treasure is buried."

"But, Danny, the map shows exactly where it is."

"What map?"

"*This* map," Tess said, whipping out another sheet of tattered parchment encased in plastic. "The one that marks seven areas and gives explicit directions to where treasure was stashed. The one that says: 'Some of these I buried myself during the time my commune at Campeche was flourishing, and others were hidden for me by my good and trusted friends, the Bowie brothers.' "

Dan looked stunned. "Let me see that." He reached toward the map.

She held the map away from him and tilted her nose in the air. "Oh, I think not. If you will excuse me, I'm going to take a shower."

Tess fluttered her fingers in a farewell gesture and strolled from the room, taking the map with her.

"Tess, come back here!" Dan roared. But she ignored him and hurried upstairs to her spacious third floor bedroom.

She'd barely locked the door behind her when Dan started rapping on it, demanding to talk to her. Stifling a giggle, she sauntered to her desk and laid the map beside Casey Prophet's journal and the other material she'd been collecting. *Serves him right for being such a spoilsport*, she thought, listening to him knock and call to her. It would do him good to stew for a while.

Daniel Friday might as well begin learning right now that he should never *ever* underestimate her.

At dinner that night, the excitement was running high as they started making plans for the treasure hunt. Everyone was talking at once. Everyone except Dan. He sat picking at the casserole Ivan had left for them.

"I just know we'll find it. Providence had a hand in this," chattered Martha Craven. "Why just the weekend before I found the journals, Olivia and I were at Delta Downs and found out Pirate's Pleasure was for sale. We were wishing we could buy him, weren't we, Olivia?"

Olivia nodded. "He reminded me of a thoroughbred my granddaddy used to have. Pirate's Bounty, his name was. Fast as the wind. When we investigated, we found out that that Pirate's Pleasure's bloodlines could be traced back to that very same horse."

"What in the world would you two do with a racehorse?" Dan asked.

"Why"—Olivia's face was perfectly straight—"we'd planned to tether him in the backyard and sell rides on him for a dollar."

Dan looked appalled.

"Miss Olivia's pulling your leg," Hook told Dan, his gold tooth flashing as he grinned. "Don't let her fool you. Miss Olivia's a fine businesswoman and she knows horses. Had a bunch of winners last year. She's got a nice little string of fillies on her farm in Louisiana, and she's had her eye out for a good stallion for stud."

Tess couldn't resist a satisfied smirk and a smug

little dip of her chin. "Jumping to conclusions about people will get you every time, Friday."

"Danny, we'll need to get the RV right away. Would you take care of transferring the cash to my checking account?"

"If you're sure that's what you want," Dan said, "but I don't understand why you need an RV, Gram."

"Tess says that we'll be much more comfortable with a portable place to rest and refresh ourselves while we're searching for the treasure. We thought about renting one, but if we buy Pirate's Pleasure, we'll be following the races more. Most of the owners have RVs at the track since they're so convenient."

"I see."

Tess was beginning to feel a little sorry for Dan. At every turn, his misgivings had been countered. "I'll get the dessert," she said, pushing away from the table.

"I'll help you." Dan followed her into the kitchen. "Tess, we need to talk."

She sliced the pound cake and distributed it to the dessert plates, then leaned back against the counter. "Dan, I know you still probably think this treasure hunt is bunk, but trust me, I've researched it very carefully for a long time. The authentication from Dr. Staats was simply a final verification of what I already knew."

"I'll admit I still think the whole idea seems far-fetched, but I'm more interested in talking about us." He wrapped his fingers around the side of her neck and stroked the edge of her jaw with his thumb. "We have some unfinished business to discuss."

He was so close that she could feel the heat from his body, and his blue-gray gaze was on her mouth. Her lips tingled and she parted them to moisten them with her tongue. His fingers tightened around her neck and he pulled her closer.

"Do you have any idea of what just the scent of you does to me, Tess?"

She shook her head slowly. "Tell me," she whispered, her voice husky.

"It sets me on fire."

He was lowering his mouth to hers when a voice said, "Oops!"

They both turned to see the flash of Olivia's long red hair and green dress as she slipped back out of the kitchen.

Dan smiled. "Later."

She chuckled, then turned and ladled lemon-butter sauce over the cake slices. When Dan helped her carry the plates to the dining room, Martha and Olivia, who had their heads together, ceased their whispering and jumped apart. Tess could almost see canary feathers dangling from the mouths of the two smiling ladies whose eyes darted back and forth between Tess and Dan.

Tess rose from the tub where she'd been soaking in a warm bubble bath and dried off. Wrapping the towel around her, she went to the door, opened it, and poked her head out, listening. The late-night news had been over for half an hour and the house was quiet. Not even the usual drone of Johnny Carson and his guests marred the silence. She smiled and closed the door.

What did one wear to a seduction?

Particularly when the seducer might meet a restless chaperone while sneaking in or out of the house? That precaution eliminated some of her more obvious choices. And it was a bit nippy out for some of the things she had considered. With a wicked grin, she finally settled on a slinky silk robe in pulsating purple. It was split up each side, cut low in front, and decorated with a long gold tassel attached to its zipper. Dan was good with zippers.

Grinning as she dressed, she thought of how surprised Dan would be when she showed up on his doorstep in nothing but a whisper of silk and a smile. He'd never be able to resist; she was going to turn his libido every which way but loose.

Tess picked up the map and the journal and, carrying her slippers in her hand, quietly tiptoed downstairs. She paused at the second floor landing to listen. The only sound she heard was the tick of the grandfather clock in the hallway below. She shrugged and, descending close to the wall to avoid squeaks and creaks, stole down the stairs and out the back door.

She stopped to pull on her slippers, then made her way to the guest cottage. The short hairs on her neck prickled and she glanced over her shoulder. A movement at a second floor window of the big house made her freeze. She could have sworn that a curtain had fluttered, but she saw nothing.

How silly, she scolded herself. She was acting like a guilty teenager. Certainly Aunt Olivia wouldn't care if she visited a man alone at night, even if she knew Tess's purpose. In her day, her aunt had been quite a coquette, and she was extremely broad-minded. But Dan's grandmother was another matter. She seemed a bit more old-fashioned than Olivia, and Tess didn't want to embarrass Aunt Martha.

Waiting in the shadows and staring at the window until she was sure that the movement had been a figment of her imagination, Tess bit back a nervous giggle. The whole thing was beginning to feel like a scene from a Pink Panther movie. Her heart was racing and she could feel the flush of excitement on her cheeks.

She only hoped that Dan wouldn't throw her out. She'd given him a hard time after dinner. Instead of maneuvering for a way to talk with him privately, she'd insisted that they join Olivia and Martha for a few rubbers of bridge. Dan hadn't been able to concentrate on the game at all; the two older ladies had thoroughly trounced them. Perhaps it was because Tess had kicked off her sandals and run her toes up his leg while they played. The first time it happened, he'd made a funny strangling sound and trumped her ace.

Grinning as she remembered the look on his face, she went to the door of the cottage and stepped out of her dew-dampened slippers. Her hand was raised to knock when the door swung open.

Her eyes glazed and her mouth went dry.

Soft music was playing inside, and there, outlined in the dim lamplight of the living room, stood Dan. Leaning with one hand on the knob and the other on his out-thrust hip, he wore the low-slung bottoms of the loden green silk pajamas she'd bought for him. She'd had an idea those pajamas would look good on him. They did. They were dynamite. If the women of America could see him now, by noon tomorrow there wouldn't be another pair of pegged silk pajama bottoms left in the country.

His feet were bare and only a patch of light brown hair curled over the muscles on his chest. His hair on his head looked damp and slightly mussed, as if he'd run his fingers through it a few times while he waited for her.

A slow smile lifted the corners of his lips, and his eyes flashed silver in the soft light as they flicked over her. "I thought you'd never get here, love." His words were a deep, rumbling caress.

"How did you know I was coming?"

His smile widened and he reached for the side of her neck and pulled her toward him. "I'm beginning to understand how your mind works." He bent and brushed his lips against hers.

"I brought the map and journal to show you."

His eyes never leaving hers, his hand still stroking her neck, he took the documents that she clutched against her breasts and laid them on a table. "The only treasure I'm interested in now is you."

He pulled her into the room and closed the door. Both arms went around her, one across her back, the other, lower to pull her hips against him. Tess almost purred as he nuzzled and nibbled the side of her throat. His hands slid over the soft silk of her robe as he rubbed his chest against hers and made soft, sensual sounds deep in his throat. Shivers rippled over her skin.

"What do you have on under this, love?"

She laughed a deep, husky laugh. "Only Opium and me."

His mouth opened over hers with a low growl, and staid Daniel Friday went wild. Her knees buckled as he thrust his tongue between her lips, retreated and thrust again. His kiss was wet and hot and hard and his hands roved all over her. It was like standing in a summer storm of sensual fury. She whimpered and he went wilder.

His broad hand slid between their bodies and pressed upward in a slow, firm stroke until he reached the swell of her breasts. He tested and explored and teased its sensitive fullness until her spine undulated like a serpent's as she strained toward the delicious sensations his fingers created.

A hiss of the zipper and his hand was against her bare flesh. He moaned; she moaned. And his tongue went deeper.

He tore his mouth away and looked down to the deep V where his hand cupped her breast and brushed its hardened tip back and forth against his chest. Her eyes followed his and she watched as he pushed the silk from her other breast and cupped and stroked it as well. She trembled as an aching need began to blossom in her body.

She raised her slumberous eyes to his. The silvery blue band had narrowed around a dark core.

"God, but you're beautiful," he murmured. "I never dreamed that any woman could be so perfect. I want to see all of you. Now."

The zipper hissed again and he stepped back. Tess shrugged her shoulders and the silk slithered down her body and draped itself into a purple pool at her feet. She could almost feel the heat on her skin as his gaze caressed the length of her.

"Oh, my *Lord*." She could see his chest heave as he sucked in great gulps of air.

"Dan?" she whispered. "Is something wrong?"

"Wrong?" He gave a wry half laugh and his gaze slid over her again. Not one dip or curve did he miss. Her breasts swelled and her belly contracted under his hot scrutiny. "Sweetheart, you're beyond my sweetest fantasy. One look at you and I'm about to go up in smoke."

"So?" She licked her lips, smiled, and, with a provocative little rotation of her torso, she stepped toward him.

"I want you so badly that I'm about to explode, and I don't want to hurry. First I want my hands and my mouth on every magnificent inch of your luscious body. I want to taste and tongue and feel and smell. I don't want to miss a single spot."

His words flashed sparks that raced through her blood and ignited a flame deep inside her. Never in her life had she wanted a man the way she wanted Dan. Never had she felt so wanton or uninhibited. It was as if they had been born for one another, and she'd been waiting for him her whole life.

Her back arched and she breathed a low, sexy laugh. "I want you to be able to take all the time you need. I don't want to miss a minute of it." She smiled, took another step forward, and reached for him.

"Tess!" He groaned and, shuddering, clutched her to him like a dying man.

Seven

Tess was a writhing mass of nerve endings as she lay on the big bed. Dan had kissed and licked and nuzzled his way from her toes to her forehead, then turned her on her stomach and started over again. Her body had yielded all its secrets to him. In his slow, sensuous quest he had explored every square millimeter of her, and he'd found erogenous zones she hadn't dreamed existed. It was exquisite torment.

"Dan," she pleaded, breathless with longing. "I can't take much more of this."

He chuckled as his tongue did lovely things to her back. "You should never have let me get my second wind." His arm and leg held her immobile while his free hand teased the sensitive flesh of her inner thigh.

"*Please*, I'm dying."

Gently, he rolled her onto her back. His eyes were bright with tender ardor as he smoothed the dark waves from her brow. "Then let's die together."

"Dan," she whimpered, reaching for his hips to pull him to her.

His control was about to blow all to hell as he looked into her magical eyes, heavy with the passion he'd stirred in them, and saw her lips ripe and swollen from his kisses. He loved Tess Cameron with every cell of his being. He didn't give a damn if he was nothing more to her than a stray she'd brought home. He ached to bury himself in her beautiful soul.

Sweat popped out on his forehead as he knelt between those gorgeous long legs. Her skin shone with the damp fever his mouth and hands had kindled, and it felt like warm satin under his fingers as they slid over the curve of her hips to cup and lift the shapely swell of her buttocks. He tried to enter her slowly, to take her tenderly, but the moment he felt the hot wetness of her, when her legs clamped around his waist, he was lost.

Their joining was a primitive, frenzied dance of hard thrusts and grinding hips and clutching hands and reaching, straining, straining.

She arched her back, cried his name, and convulsed with such a sweet throbbing that he was carried over the edge.

She pulled him against her sweat-slicked breasts and they lay silent, sated, for long moments.

"Oh, Tess. My Tess." He stroked her and murmured soft endearments as their breathing gradually slowed. He started to roll away, to take his weight from her, but she held him fast.

"Stay," she whispered. "Stay."

Sometime near dawn Dan awoke. "What are you doing?"

Tess giggled. "I'm nibbling your toes."

He laughed. "Come here."

Tess nearly had a stroke when she saw the sun streaming between the blinds. She glanced at the bedside clock. It was almost nine! She'd meant to leave and be back in her room before dawn. Throwing back the covers, she tried to get out of bed, but Dan had both arms around her and one leg thrown over hers. He tightened his hold when she moved.

"Where are you going?" he mumbled, half awake.

"It's almost nine o'clock. I've got to get out of here."

"No, you don't." He nuzzled her neck and trailed the tip of his tongue along her shoulder. "I have a better idea."

"Dan, please don't." She wiggled under the taunting ministrations of his mouth. "I've got to go. What about your grandmother?"

"She can get her own fellow." His tongue snaked a shivering path down her spine.

"Dannnn!" she squealed as his hand slipped between her thighs.

It was ten o'clock before she tried to sneak in the back door of the big house. Ivan called to her from the kitchen. He was grinning from ear to ear and he wiggled one bushy eyebrow. It was obvious that he'd seen her come from the guest cottage. The kitchen window provided an unobstructed view of Dan's front door. He'd probably seen the steamy kiss that Dan had planted on her as well.

"You want some breakfast? Shall I make French toast?"

Tess gathered her dignity and clutched the front

of her rumpled silk robe. "Not right now, thanks. When did you get home?"

"Only a moment ago. My seminar was a great success!"

"Great," Tess said distractedly. "Where are Aunt Olivia and Aunt Martha?"

He shrugged. "They're not here. I thought they were with you, but—" He grinned and wiggled his eyebrows again.

"Hook probably took them shopping for an RV." Relieved at her reprieve, Tess started to make a hasty exit to her room, then stopped. "Ivan, not a word of this to anybody."

He put his hand on his chest. "My lips are sealed."

Tess was dressed and coming down the stairs when Olivia, Martha, and Hook came in the door. Hook was carrying Martha, whose left foot and ankle were swathed in an elastic bandage.

"What happened?" Tess asked, concerned when she saw the wrapping.

"Oh, nothing to be alarmed about," Olivia said, waving a dismissing hand. "Martha twisted her ankle. The doctor said it's just a sprain, but she must stay off of it for a week or two." She heaved a sigh. "Of course this means that we can't go with you on the treasure hunt. Martha must rest and keep her foot up, and I must nurse her."

"I feel simply terrible about it," Martha said, heaving a sigh of her own. "I suppose we won't need the RV for a while yet if Olivia and I aren't going. But Tess, this mustn't stop you. I know you haven't much longer on the option for your house. I'm sure Danny would go with you and help."

"That's a wonderful idea," Olivia said. "This afternoon Hook can gather everything you'll need, and the two of you could start first thing tomorrow morning."

Hook grinned and his gold tooth sparkled. "No problem. I'll even loan you my truck."

Early the next morning, as they drove Hook's Bronco across the long causeway spanning the bay, Tess said, "Are you sure you want to do this?"

Dan laughed. "Is the pope Catholic?"

She smiled. "Where have I heard that before? Seriously, Dan, I know how you feel about the treasure."

"That was before I read your great-great-grandmother's journal. After studying her account, I believe that there was once something there. Whether it's there now—" He shrugged. "In any case, I couldn't let you go anywhere without me." Taking one hand from the steering wheel, he reached across the seat and gave Tess's hand a squeeze. "Having you all to myself for a few days is like a gift from heaven."

"I feel awful about leaving Aunt Olivia and your grandmother. They'd counted on coming along to find the treasure. It was to have been a great adventure for them. They were terribly disappointed. We'd been planning our trek for weeks. Maybe we should wait until Aunt Martha's ankle is healed. I felt so sorry for her standing on the porch with her cane and waving her handkerchief good-bye to us that I almost cried."

Dan chortled. "Don't feel sorry for that cotton-topped scamp. Or for her red-haired cohort."

Tess was shocked by Dan's insensitivity to his grandmother's pain and told him so.

Dan merely chuckled. "Did you notice which ankle

she had bandaged this morning as she hobbled around so pathetically?"

Frowning, she pondered for a minute. "The right one, I think."

He nodded. "It was. Yesterday it was the left."

Tess sat up straight. "That old faker! Why would she do a thing like that?"

Amused, he said, "I think our relatives are playing Cupid. They're giving us a few days alone." He wiggled her fingers playfully and winked at her. "Mind?"

Tess grinned and looked him up and down lasciviously. "I'll bite the bullet."

Dan threw back his head and laughed.

Soon they turned off the interstate and on to another highway which would lead them north through LaPorte and Baytown to east Texas. While Dan drove, Tess read the road map spread out over the knees of her jeans and acted as navigator, pointing out various sights along the way. The original map and journal had been left in Galveston, but photocopies of those documents lay in the seat beside her.

"Where to first?" Dan asked.

Tess picked up the copy of her treasure map with the seven spots marked in red. Tapping the eraser of her pencil against her chin, she said, "Casey and Marsh Prophet found the seventh one near San Augustine." She crossed it off. "And we now that the first cache was buried on the property where the house is now." She made an X through the first spot and chuckled. "Wouldn't the town's founding fathers have had a fit if they'd known what was buried on the lot they sold in 1838 for four hundred dollars?"

"Was that the property Violet's father deeded to her when she married?"

"Yes. Actually there were two pieces. The other was a waterfront property where Violet's husband, James Kirby, built a warehouse for his shipping business." She marked out another spot. "According to Casey's journal, her grandparents, Violet and James, recovered the second stash after the Civil War. It was buried on the site of Champ d'Asile, a French settlement on the Trinity River. From what I can find out, Laffite gave the group some assistance and was friendly with the leaders, who were generals exiled after Waterloo, but the settlement wasn't successful and they abandoned the site a year or two before Laffite left Galveston. Now nobody's exactly sure where the colony once was." She looked up and grinned. "Think we should tell them?"

Dan laughed. "I think it would be wise to leave it alone. Which one is next?"

"The Cherry Cemetery at Atascosito, near the town of Liberty."

"The one where a gravedigger suddenly disappeared and later turned up in San Francisco as a millionaire?" Dan chuckled. "Like your granny Mrs. Prophet, I think we can safely assume that he dug up more than dirt. I wonder who he was digging the grave for?"

Tess ruffled through the papers beside her and pulled out one. "Zelda Marie Gossett, age seventy-six." She looked over at Dan, an impish gleam in her eye. Although he was good-naturedly going along with her scheme, she suspected that he was still skeptical. Perhaps validating some of the facts in the hundred forty-year-old journal would help dispel any lingering doubts. "Why don't we stop by and check it out? The cemetery is just up the road from the library and museum where Laffite's journal is displayed. It's not far."

An hour later they were standing in front of a glass case that held the original diary. Tess glanced around to make sure they were alone in the small museum, then pulled a copy of the letter from "Theodore Lucas" out of her leather portfolio.

"Look," she whispered, holding the sheet next to the worn volume. "Anybody can see that the handwriting is the same."

Dan looked from the letter to the faded pages protected by the glass case, then back to Tess. He smiled and dropped a kiss on her nose. "I believe you, honey." Lacing his fingers through hers, they wandered to the next display, peering at pictures of Jean Laffite, alias John Lafflin, and family from his later years in St. Louis.

After they left the building, they drove up the hill to a cemetery shaded by a small grove of trees on a high land rise. They walked slowly among the stones, many weathered and dim, others newer and deeply chiseled.

As they searched, Tess said, "The man who originally owned his land was a good friend of Laffite's. I suppose he continued to use this place as a cemetery after Laffite asked to bury 'one of his men' on the hill."

"Probably." Dan squatted by an old marker and ran his fingers over the words. "Here it is. *Zelda Marie Gossett, born February 10, 1816, died April 18, 1882.* Casey Prophet was only six years too late to find the place. I wonder what happened to the original stone that marked the place where he buried the treasure?" He stood, dusted his hands on his jeans, and put his arm around Tess as they both looked down at the ground where a fortune in gold and gems had once been secreted.

"I don't know. His description says it was a granite cross with vines and blossoms carved across its surface."

Tess slid her arm around Dan's waist and leaned her head against his shoulder as they stood on the hill and surveyed the gently rolling land below. Only the occasional twitter of birds and the faint buzz of insects in the grass entered the quiet. A fresh spring breeze rose and rustled through the grove of trees, swaying the branches and whispering and hissing among the leaves, as if to tease them with its secrets. It blew over the fields of yellow wildflowers growing in the meadows and moved across the land so that the simple blossoms rippled like a vast, softly waving sea of sunshine.

"Isn't it beautiful?" she asked. "It must have been about this time of year that he was here. He said that, in the springtime, the cross overlooked a yellow sea." She shivered and Dan hugged her close, running his hands over her arms.

"Cold?"

Tess shook her head. "Awed, I think. He must have stood on this very spot a hundred and seventy years ago. He must have watched the procreators of these very flowers." She snuggled close to the strong man whose presence warmed her inside and out. "Oh, Dan, I just know we're going to find the treasure. He meant for us to find it."

Dan lifted her face and looked into her eyes. He smiled and brushed a few wind-tossed strands of hair from her face. "I've found my treasure."

He bent and kissed her with a tenderness that brought tears shimmering to the edge of her lids as they fluttered and closed. She sighed, slipped her arms around his neck, and returned his kiss. Never had any moment been so perfect. Never had anything felt so right.

"Let me handle this," Dan said out of the side of his mouth as they walked into the records office at the Polk County courthouse.

As they entered, a middle-aged woman, whose dark brows were arched in a thin line of perpetual surprise, looked up from her sandwich. She smiled and wiped her fingers on a paper napkin. "What can I do for you folks today?"

Dan smiled and stuck out his hand. "I'm Daniel Friday from Pittsburgh, Pennsylvania. And this is my wife, Tess."

His wife? Tess resisted the urge to elbow him in the ribs.

The lady took his hand and returned his smile. "Della Boynton. Assistant County Clerk." She nodded to Tess.

"My grandmother is working on our family's genealogy, and we promised to stop by while we were on our vacation and get some information for her. I hope you can help." Charm oozed from him.

The clerk patted the back of her short curls, which were a bright shade of red somewhere between Lucille Ball's and Aunt Olivia's. "Why, I'll be happy to do what I can. I'm interested in genealogy myself. What do you need?"

Out of his pocket, Dan pulled a slip of paper with the information Tess had written on it. "In the eighteen-eighties, a man named Nathan Power owned a farm near the Trinity River. He was a cousin on my great-grandfather Power's side. We'd like to know where it's located and if any of the family still owns the property. My grandmother has a diary that her father wrote telling about the beauty of the land there. We promised her that we'd stop by and see it and take some pictures for her." Dan smiled again.

Della smiled back and Tess rolled her eyes heavenward. Dan was spreading it on by the shovelful. But, she had to hand it to him. It seemed to be working.

The thought that they might be getting close pumped a shot of adrenaline into Tess's bloodstream that tripped her heartbeat into doubletime and brought a flush of excitement to her face. The Prophets had discovered that the fourth site was under Nathan Power's chicken house. After they discovered that the fourth site was under Nathan Power's chicken coop, Power had sicced his dogs on them and the Prophets had left. The chicken coop was sure to be gone and the old codger had long since met his maker, but Tess knew where the landmarks were. She crossed her fingers behind her back and made a silent entreaty.

"Why, sure thing," Della said, patting the back of her hair again. "It's slower than Dish Taylor's coon hound around here today. Why don't y'all have some lunch and come back in about two hours? That should give me enough time. I'll copy everything your granny might like to have for her research, too. Fifty cents a page."

They found a little café off the square and slid into the red plastic booth. When the waitress brought them water and menus, Tess took a medicine bottle from her purse and shook a tablet into Dan's hand.

After he downed it, Dan smiled. "You should have been a nurse."

"Not me. I can't stand the sight of blood." Looking up from the menu, she said, "I know you don't like to talk about it, but are you having any trouble with your stomach?"

He shook his head. "It hasn't bothered me in a couple of weeks. Taking time off from the company, staying in Galveston . . . being with you, Tess . . . especially being with you"—he took her hand and rubbed his thumb across her palm—"has been the best thing that could have happened to me. Getting sick was worth it. I would have risked a hundred ulcers for the chance to meet you."

His smile, his touch, his words sent ripples of pleasure over her. Her voice was husky with emotion when she tried to answer. "Dan, I—"

"You folks ready to order?" The waitress stood poised with a pencil and order pad.

"Give us another few minutes," Dan said, releasing Tess's hand. When the woman left, he asked, "I don't suppose I could talk you into a greasy, juicy hamburger and french fries, could I?"

Tess laughed. "Not on your life. I'm thinking more along the lines of macaroni and cheese and green beans."

He breathed a long-suffering sigh. "I was afraid of that."

They decided on lunch, and when the food was brought, Tess only pushed hers around on the plate.

"Nervous?" Dan asked.

"Excited." She put her fork down. "Maybe 'antsy' is a better description. I've dreamed of living in that house since I was a little girl. Dan, I can't explain to you how I feel about it. Obsessed, maybe. It's always fascinated me, drawn me into a kind of spell as if its rusticated walls are magical. Even as an adult, after

I came to realize that it was out of my price range, somewhere inside of me, there has always been a secret longing to have all those gables and towers and wonderfully carved corbels for my very own. I've spent hours looking at it, wandering through it, dreaming about it. Does that sound crazy?"

He reached for her hand and smiled. "Not at all."

"I can picture how exquisite it will be when it's restored. Now, because of a man who was born two hundred years ago, we can make it beautiful." She squeezed his hand and beamed with bubbling anticipation. "My fantasy is about to come true. I can hardly wait."

"Tess—"

Her smile faded. "Yes?" Her tone was a warning.

"Eat your squash."

Tess and Dan stood on the bank staring out over the ninety thousand-acre Lake Livingston, seventy-five square miles of deep, green, murky water. In the distance a speed boat roared across its surface with a skier in tow.

"Oh, Dan," Tess wailed, burying her face against his shoulder. "I was hoping Della Boynton had made a mistake."

He rocked her back and forth and patted her back. "I'm sorry, honey, but it looks like Nate Power's chicken house is in the middle of the lake under fifty feet of water."

"How could they do this?"

He shrugged helplessly. "Progress?"

An idea occurred to her and she drew back, excited. "We can hire a team of divers."

Dan shook his head and kissed her nose. "Sweetheart, the landmarks are gone, too, and all we have is a general idea of which two hundred acres the farm was. It's impossible."

Tess sighed and wiped her eyes. "Damn! And after you paid Della twenty-three dollars for that stack of deeds and plats and tax roll lists."

He smiled and they walked back to the Bronco. "Why don't we drive on to Lufkin, find a motel, and get a fresh start in the morning?"

"A motel?" She raised an eyebrow. "One room?"

"One room."

Tess laughed. "Let's go."

Sometime after midnight, Dan awoke. He missed the warmth of Tess's body next to his. His hand searched the empty space of the king-size bed.

"Tess?"

"I'm here," she whispered from the shadows.

"What are you doing out of bed?" He got up and went to the window where she stood naked, staring out the blinds at the distorted reflection of the motel's neon sign on the swimming pool.

"Just thinking, planning. I didn't mean to wake you. I couldn't sleep."

He stood behind her, wrapped his arms around her, and rubbed his face in the fragrance of her silky hair. "I'm getting used to having you beside me. I miss you when you're gone."

Crossing her arms over his, she absently rubbed his arm.

"What are you thinking about?" he asked.

"Lots of things."

"The treasure?"

She nodded. "I wonder what it will look like and

how we'll dispose of it. The booty the Prophets found in the seventh place near San Augustine was four metal chests full. Some of it was gold coins, some was in gold and silver bars, and some was jewelry and precious stones. If we find gold coins, I imagine that the collector's value will be greater than the weight-value of the gold."

"I imagine."

Dan rested his cheek against the crown of her head and savored her sweet scent and the feel of her bare skin against his. His heart ached for her. He knew that the chances of their finding anything after all this time were almost non-existent—even a hundred years ago the Prophets had only been able to recover the goods from one site—but he couldn't bring himself to dash her hopes. When she talked about the treasure, the look of joyful anticipation on her face was worth all the gold in the world.

A part of him wanted her to be able to hang on to her dream as long as she could. He understood about dreams.

But another part of him—the pragmatic part—wanted her to abandon her search before she had to face the pain and reality of coming up empty.

All he could do was go with her and stand by her and love her enough to ease some of the disappointment she was bound to suffer when the fifth and sixth spots on the map yielded nothing. When this thing was over, and she was finally satisfied that there was no treasure to buy a decrepit castle in Galveston, he would take her back to Pittsburgh with him. Because of Tess, he'd already stayed longer than the month he'd promised himself. After they were married, he would even build her an exact replica of her beautiful-ugly mansion. Hell, he'd buy the damned thing in Galveston and have it shipped stone by stone to Pennsylvania if that's what it would take to make her happy. He couldn't think of anything he wouldn't do for Tess.

"Tess?"

"Hmmmm?" She leaned her head back against his shoulder as he nuzzled the satin-soft skin at the pulse point of her neck.

"I love you."

She turned in his arms and looked up at him. Even in the dim light he could see the beauty of her smile. It bathed the darkness with sunshine and warmed his blood.

"Dan?"

"Hmmmm?"

"I love you, too."

Eight

The clerk at the Angelina County courthouse was busier than Della but just as helpful. And to Tess's everlasting relief, as far as they could determine, the area they were looking for this time was not underwater. By early afternoon, they were headed to the fifth spot, located several miles outside of Lufkin, a small town in the piny woods of central east Texas.

"Are you sure we shouldn't ask the lumber company that owns the property for permission to nose around?" Dan asked.

Tess shook her head. "The clerk said they own acres and acres in that area. I doubt that anyone connected with the company will even know that we're there." She checked the journal pages again. "According to Casey's account, a church had been built on the site a few years before they found it, and when she and Marsh came through looking for the treasure, the community had gathered for a week-long revival meeting after spring planting. Some of the more distant families were camped on the grounds and, since there wasn't room to dig under the church even if all those people hadn't been around, they moved on."

Dan stared at her in disbelief. "Do you mean for us to crawl under an old church and start digging holes?"

She laughed. "The church isn't there anymore. In my preliminary research, I discovered that it burned down in 1896 and was never rebuilt. Turn here," she said, indicating a dirt road on their right, which was little more than shallow ruts.

After they had bumped down the road for about a mile and a half, they pulled to a stop and studied the maps and notes Tess had assembled in a file folder labeled "Five."

"The church was somewhere in this area." Dan tapped a spot on the map he held. "We should be close if the Bowie brothers buried it south of where the springs rise to form this branch. I'm surprised that the old pirate trusted them with so much loot."

"Privateer," she corrected automatically. "And apparently he did. They were longtime friends and business associates. I doubt that he trusted lightly. Let's see if we can find the stream and then we can follow it back."

When they got out of the Bronco, Tess was almost giddy with anticipation. Dan laced his fingers through hers. "You're trembling."

"I'm excited. Have you got the compass?" He nodded and smiled indulgently. She laughed and tugged at his hand. "Come on. I can't wait."

As they walked through the woods, redolent with pine and the fresh scents of newly leafed sweet gum, sassafras, oak, and hickory trees, Tess could barely contain her exuberance. She felt like dancing to the sound of the twittering birds overhead; she felt as if she would have flown over the treetops if Dan weren't holding on to her hand. She was close. *So close.*

Ducking under low-hanging branches, she ignored the vines and underbrush plucking at their jeans as they trekked over the newest layer of pine needles and deteriorating leaves. Now and then there was a skittering rustle in the bushes as if the rabbits and squirrels were clearing a path for their guest.

Her thoughts were bumping into each other as she hurried in the direction of what she was sure smelled and sounded like water.

Suddenly, her right foot felt only empty space beneath it. She pitched forward, but Dan caught her and hauled her back. She had nearly plunged over the bank of a small creek.

"Hold it, woman," Dan said, laughing and hugging her to him. "You almost got a dunking."

Her eyes widened and her heart was racing like a runaway train. When she recovered her wits, she squealed, "Oh, Dan, we found it!" She threw her arms around him and planted a smacking kiss in the general vicinity of his mouth.

"We've found the branch," he reminded her. "We haven't found the spring or the treasure."

"But we will," she said, grabbing his hand and charging upstream. "We will."

They had tracked only about fifty yards when Tess saw something and stopped dead still. Not more than twenty feet ahead stood the distinctive rock and the headwaters of the branch. Her heart was in her throat and an eerie rush swept over her. "Look," she whispered, pointing with one shaking finger to the spot shaded by dense foliage.

The twisted trunk of a late-blooming dogwood tree,

its branches in full white flower, clung to the earth and draped its limbs over a huge, rust-colored rock. Beneath the rock, which rose from a thick cluster of deep green wood fern, was an embankment of striated clay in putty gray and rust brown hues. In several areas along the four-foot bank, shaped by eons of wellspring erosion, water trickled from unseen crevices and gathered in a stream. It trilled, glass-clear, over a bed strewn with pebbles and rippled from years of washing. So pure and cool did the water appear that it seemed to invite them to dip their hands in and drink.

Smells of cool, damp clay, warming humus, and the pungent crispness of verdant growth hung in the sheltered thicket of old trees and ancient springs, entreating Tess to breathe in their sensual essence.

"How *beautiful*," she whispered again.

Dan stood beside her, looking more at her than at the sight which had enchanted her. "Beautiful."

Tess smiled. "This is the rock he described. These are the springs. They must be. The Bowie brothers must have camped beside this very spot."

"Think we'll find one of Jim Bowie's old knives around?" Dan teased.

"Not likely." Tess gave him a little pinch on the belly as she beamed with excitement, "but I suspect we're about to find something even better. Taking his hand, she pulled him toward the rock. "Come on."

After Dan brushed aside the branches of the dogwood tree so that she could stand flush against the rock, he broke off a small sprig of the white blossoms and tucked them behind her ear.

He stood facing her, one arm holding back the limbs that framed her with delicate blooms, the other hand at her neck. His thumb stroked the curve of her jaw. "I don't think you've ever seemed so lovely or so precious to me as you do now, Tess."

"Because I'm about to be rich with Jean Laffite's gold?" She gave him a saucy grin.

"No." He shook his head slowly.

"Then it must be my fetching outfit," she said, plucking at the front of her turquoise jersey, which had an advertisement for the Mermaid emblazoned in purple across her chest.

"No." He grinned and dropped his hand to trace the mermaid's tail that ended just at the inner swell of her right breast. "Though it is extremely provocative."

At Dan's touch, a rash of goose bumps prickled over her skin, and she smiled. "Then why?"

He kissed her lightly. "I suppose it's because each day I see more of your spirit and love you more. I've never known anyone like you, Tess. You're unique. And very, very special." He kissed her again, gently. "Gold or no gold, purple jeans or Paris silks, I cherish you, love. I don't want anything to hurt you, ever."

Her smile widened. "I think I like being cherished."

He tweaked her nose and chuckled. "You should." Reaching in his pocket, he pulled out the compass and looked down at it. "Are you sure you want to do this?"

"I'm sure."

He handed the instrument to her. "One hundred paces, due south." Still holding the branches away from her, he stepped aside.

Her fingers closed around the compass and she could feel a similar constriction in her throat. She was excited and a little scared. Her insides felt like a sack of agitated bumble bees.

What if the treasure wasn't there? No. She wouldn't allow such thoughts to enter her mind. It *was* there. It had to be.

Looking down at the needle to get her bearings, she shifted her position slightly. She squeezed her eyes shut and took a deep breath.

"Here goes." She squared her shoulders and took the first step. "One," she said as she began to count her strides. "Two."

When she had moved away from the branches of the dogwood, Dan paced beside her, clearing her path of low-hanging limbs and steering her around trees and bushes while she kept her eyes on the compass and counted.

"Ninety-nine . . . one hundred."

Tess stopped and looked up. The spot where she was standing seemed no different from the rest of the wooded area. For some reason she was disappointed. It was irrational, since the church had been gone for almost ninety years, but she had expected to find a clearing or at least something significant to indicate that a fortune rested in the ground beneath her feet.

"I'll mark the place," Dan said. He pulled a white handkerchief from his back pocket and tied it to a bush about a foot to the right of where she stood.

She didn't move. "What now?"

Dan smiled and took her hand. "Let's look around." They searched in widening circles with Dan studying the ground and stopping occasionally to scrape the leaves aside with the side of his boot.

"What are we looking for?" Tess whispered when he squatted down to examine a pile of rust-colored rocks.

Standing, he dusted his hands on his jeans and chuckled. "Why are you whispering?"

Tess shrugged her shoulders. "I don't know. Something about the place and the occasion seems to inspire reverence, I suppose. What are we looking for?"

"I'll show you." He walked a few yards to another tumbled pile of rocks and pointed to them.

She looked at the rocks and back to Dan. "So?"

"So, I suspect that these piles of rocks were once used as piers to support the lumber girders of the church building."

"Ah," she said, understanding. "The church was here." She grinned. "You're handy to have around. Let's get the metal detector and the shovels."

"You stay here and I'll move the truck closer and get the things we'll need." He gave her a quick kiss and struck off through the trees to the road.

Tess sat down on the pile of rocks and, elbows on her knees and chin on her fists, stared at the white handkerchief tied to the bush. Three feet under the ground were old metal chests which would provide Aunt Olivia and Aunt Martha their racehorse and Tess with her dream castle.

She closed her eyes and envisioned the way each room would look when it was finished. She could imagine Dan and herself working on the plans, watching the changes as the old mansion came to life again, and, finally, sitting together in the living room beside a fire in the Italian marble fireplace. The couch was huge and poofy, covered in oyster suede; the walls were blue watered silk; a magnificent Persian rug covered the polished wooden floors; a Christmas tree stood in the corner beside a long table where a gleaming brass samovar reflected the twinkling tree lights.

She could smell the wood burning, and the fragrance of evergreens and warm cinnamon and nutmeg and potpourri wafted through the high-ceilinged room. Snuggled beside Dan, she felt totally content. He would look at her, smile, and say—

"Tess!"

She startled and the image popped like a bubble.

Dan was grinning. "Where were you off to?"

She laughed. "Beside a fire in the living room. Oh, Dan, everything is going to be so fantastic." She squeezed her hands between her knees.

He drew his brows together. "Tess—"

"Yes?"

He hesitated. "Nothing. Let's check the area with the metal detector."

By dusk, Dan had dug four holes and found an old pick-ax head, part of a wagon wheel rim, a horseshoe, and the rusty remains of what looked to have once been a kettle.

He pulled off his gloves, stuck them in his back pocket, and leaned on the shovel. "We have to face it, babe. It's not here."

Chewing on her lip, Tess shifted her weight from one foot to the other as her eyes darted over the area. "You know, Jim Bowie's legs may have been longer than mine. Or shorter. We may have missed it by a few feet. Let's walk it off again. I'll take longer strides this time."

Dan caught her arm as she strode toward the springs. "Love, we've searched the entire area with the metal detector. It's not here."

"But it *has* to be!"

Dropping the shovel, he gathered her to him, hugging and soothing her with soft words of comfort. "I'm sorry, Tess. I'm sorry."

• •

By midmorning they had driven the twenty or so miles to Nacogdoches, a picturesque little place set amid gently rolling hills and red dirt, reputedly the oldest town in Texas. They checked into a hotel a block or two off the brick-paved main street.

After he'd tipped the bellman and closed the door, Dan asked, "Shall we make another trip to the county courthouse?"

"Nope." Tess smiled smugly. "Everybody knows where the Old Stone Fort is. It's on the campus of Stephen F. Austin University on the north side of town. I had some friends who went to college there, and I spent a few weekends visiting with them. Would you believe I even toured the place once? I must have been within a few feet of the spot where the treasure is buried."

Spreading a sheaf of papers on the bed, she lay down on her stomach to study them. Dan stretched out beside her and propped his head on one hand while the other stole under the hem of her red cotton sweater to lazily stroke her back. When he touched an especially sensitive spot near her right shoulder blade, she wiggled. He chuckled, leaned over, and touched the tip of his tongue to her nape.

"Dannn!" she squealed. "I'm trying to read."

"You've read those pages a hundred times," he said, laughing as he brushed the papers off the bed and pulled her on top of him. He kissed her nose. "I'll bet you can recite them verbatim, can't you?"

She grinned. "Probably. Jean Laffite had the Bowies bury this batch behind the fort, six feet out from the center of the back wall. He'd originally meant it to help finance some of the early settlers. I gather that he had 'deposited' it and was waiting to see if it would be to his advantage to loan them money. But he got ticked off at James Long, who was"—she tucked her chin and lowered her voice to speak in an exaggerated French accent—"a dishonest, land-grabbing thief who proclaimed himself Governor of Texas to lead his band of robbers."

Dan laughed. "Wasn't that the pot calling the kettle black?"

"I suppose it depends on your point of view. Long may have been considered an early Texas hero, but Laffite had nothing good to say about him. According to his journal, Long and some of his men made a mistake when they stole goods from Laffite. He had his own peculiar code of honor; I think the rascal took perverse pleasure in knowing that all the time Long and his emissaries were begging him to loan them money for armies and expeditions, they were sitting in Nacogdoches only a few feet from a fortune."

"He *was* a rascal."

"I have an idea. Why don't we go check out the fort before lunch?" Tess tried to push herself up, but Dan held her.

"I have a better idea. Why don't we—" He whispered some slightly scandalous suggestions in her ear.

Tess giggled and almost blushed as she gave him a playful swat. "You're a worse rascal than Laffite. I knew from the first time I met you there was a tiger beneath that staid exterior."

Looking pleased, Dan broke into his lopsided, boyish grin. "You think I'm a tiger, huh?" Suddenly, he snarled and flipped her on to her back, nipping and nuzzling her neck until she squealed with laughter and begged him to stop. "You bring out the animal in me," he growled, holding her down and continuing his feigned biting over her bare midriff where her sweater had ridden up.

In the space of two heartbeats, the playfulness changed to passion, the biting to trailing kisses, wet and warm across her belly as he unbuttoned the front of her denim skirt.

Tess came alive as he stroked and petted and caressed. Electricity charged her body as his tongue laved her, as his kisses covered her, as he whispered love words in her ears. Longing to have him inside her pushed away all thoughts of treasure and the dreams it fostered. Dan, the smell of him, the feel of him, the taste of him, filled her mind with a solitary splendor.

They shed their clothes and came together in a slow melding of skin on skin, giving and receiving, loving and being loved, until they lay quiet and replete in each other's arms.

"Lord, I love you," Dan said, running his hand over the curve of her hip. "Tess—" He stopped before he finished the question he was about to ask. He wanted to ask her to forget the treasure and marry him today, now, before she suffered a final disappointment. He wanted to wrap her in a charmed cocoon of protection so that she would know only joy and laughter and the fulfillment of her slightest wish. But he'd come to know Tess Cameron too well. She'd never give up without trying to find her treasure. Not when the spot lay only a few miles away. Not his Tess.

"Yes?"

"I'm hungry," he said, improvising a quick reply.

"Me, too."

They showered and dressed, then went in search

of a restaurant. After lunch, they drove to the university campus and parked near the Old Stone Fort.

Rather small and insignificant among the huge trees and modern buildings, the two-story fort was constructed of native rust red rock. Heavy wooden beams supported an open gallery off the second floor and rose to support the roof overhang as well. Tess and Dan stood in front of it and looked up at the many flags fluttering from poles mounted on the beams.

The campus was busy with cars and bikes and students going to and from afternoon classes or simply hanging out with one another on the sunny spring day.

A young man in cutoffs and a flattop had parked his convertible under a nearby tree and was waxing it. The radio was blaring hard rock, and he spread the paste to its beat. He missed a couple of licks when two shapely coeds in snug short-shorts jogged by.

Tess and Dan looked at one another and grinned.

"Ah, spring," Dan said.

"Ah, hormones." Tess laughed as they walked to the big wooden door of the fort.

It was locked. A notice posted the hours it would be open the following day. Tess shrugged. She didn't care if the museum was unavailable for viewing. Only the outside of the fort interested her. Trying to look nonchalant, she and Dan strolled around to the back. There was a small wedge of open ground, no more than seventy-five feet at its widest point, between the rear of the fort and a sprawling modern building with a large greenhouse beside it. By mutual consent, they walked the length of the rock wall, counting quietly as they went.

When they reached the corner, Tess did a little mental arithmetic and whispered, "It's twelve and a half paces to the middle."

They stepped off the distance and stood hand in hand with their backs to the wall. Tess's heart was beating so loudly that the sound of it in her ears drowned out the rock music from the radio across the way. The chicken à la king they had eaten for lunch formed a seething blob in her stomach that seemed to be creeping up her esophagus. She swallowed it back down and squeezed Dan's hand.

They took a synchronized giant step forward. Then another.

"It's here," she whispered, barely able to keep her voice down. "It's here right under our feet. We're standing on a fortune in gold." The words came out in a high little squeak.

Dan cleared his throat and cut his eyes toward a couple a few feet away. The girl was against a big elm growing beside the greenhouse, and the boy, a hand on either side of her head, was leaning on the tree. They were gazing rapturously into one another's eyes.

"I don't think they heard me," Tess whispered. "I don't think they would hear an atomic explosion on the next block."

Amusement lifted the corners of Dan's lips. "I think you're right." Taking Tess's hand, they walked to an area out of earshot. "How do you propose we dig for treasure in an area with people everywhere?"

"Simple," she answered, since she'd already considered the same complication. "We dig at night."

Just after three o'clock in the morning, the truck

rolled to a stop on a side street beside the fort. Everything was still. The place that had been alive with activity earlier in the afternoon was deserted. Streetlights lining the boulevard cast eerie shadows through the trees. Tess was so wired with adrenaline that she felt as if her heart was about to explode.

"I feel like a commando," Dan grumbled. "Or a cat burglar."

Tess stifled a giggle as she looked him over. They were dressed identically in black jeans and long-sleeved jerseys that she'd insisted they buy for the occasion. "I think you look cute." She wiggled her eyebrow, and dropped her naturally husky voice even lower to add, "Very sexy."

Smiling, he said, "Flattery will do it every time. Let's go."

"Wait! Don't forget your cap and your gloves." She thrust the dark articles at him and pulled a can of black shoe polish out of the sack she held between her legs.

"I'll wear the stupid cap," he said, stretching the knit over his head, "but I'll be damned if I'll paint my face with shoe polish."

She shrugged and slapped a few streaks on her own. "Suit yourself."

As Tess was about to open the door, a sports car roared around the corner and they slunk down in the seat. Laughter and shouting cut through the quiet, and an empty beer can clanked and rolled against the curb as the low-slung car zoomed past.

"Stupid kids," Dan mumbled. "Why are they out drinking beer at this ungodly hour? Don't they have classes in the morning? They should be home in bed."

Tess laughed. "Didn't you sow a few oats in college? Mess around on school nights just for the heck of it?"

"Not at three-thirty in the morning."

"Figures."

"What did you mean by that?"

"Friday, as adorable as you are, sometimes you can be an old coot." Tess sighed and opened the door. "Come on."

They took shovels and a flashlight from the back. "Shouldn't we take the metal detector, too?" Dan asked.

"Why? We know exactly where it is."

"I think we should check with the metal detector before we start shoveling around a state historical site."

"Bring it if you insist," she said, exasperated by his overly cautious behavior. "But *I'm* going to start digging." She stalked off through the azalea bushes to the back wall of the rock building.

Dan had seemed so different lately that she had almost forgotten about his former stuffiness. Although he'd loosened up considerably and acted more adventurously—especially in bed, she thought with a secret smile—she should have realized that bone-deep attitudes didn't disappear overnight. Oh, well, she'd have to work on him some more.

By the time she'd paced off the distance to the center of the back wall, he was beside her. Even though the rear of the fort was in shadow, her eyes had adjusted enough to the dark to dig. While he started to sweep the ground with the detector, she stuck her shovel in the hard dirt and shoved her foot against the shoulder of the blade.

"Tess, would you move the spade and wait until I check, please?" he whispered.

She sighed, stepped back a few feet, leaned against the rough wall, and waited, biting her tongue to keep from saying something really tacky.

"Well?" she asked impatiently after he'd made the third pass over the spot.

"I think there's something here." There was an incredulous tone to his whispered words.

"I told you so!"

"Shhhh."

Clamping her lips together, Tess grabbed her shovel and positioned the blade point against the packed ground. Her heart was beating so hard and fast that she could feel it pounding her ribs. Her hands were sweaty under the dark work gloves, and a little trickle of perspiration eased from her hair line and ran down her temple. She wiped it away with the sleeve of her jersey and stepped on the spade.

She shoveled, tossing the dirt over her shoulder to land in soft thuds behind her while Dan placed his in a neat, growing mound beside the hole he dug. After what seemed like two hours, but was no more than a few minutes, Tess stopped to wipe the sweat from her forehead.

Metal clinked against metal.

"I think I've hit something," Dan said.

"Oh, Dan!" she squealed, dropping her shovel and throwing her arms around him. "You've found it!"

"Shhhh. Let me clear out some more dirt."

Moving aside, she crossed fingers on both hands and prayed. It was here. It had to be here. For the first time, Tess allowed herself to admit that a niggling doubt or two had snuck into her mind since their disappointment at the site of the old church. But they'd found it! Her heart went into triple-time; her stomach constricted into knots tighter than tangled chains in a jewelry box, and her whole body trembled as Dan bent and stuck the spade into the dirt.

When the shovel scraped down the side of the hole and clanked again, she crammed her fist against her mouth to quell a whimper. She was breathing so hard and fast that she was afraid she'd keel over from hyperventilation.

A hundred years ago, the Prophets hadn't been able to recover the treasure because, according to Casey's journal, the area had been too heavily populated for them to sneak in and dig it up. There had been a boarding house and a livery stable nearby, and the old stone building had been turned into a rather bawdy saloon with a bunch of rough customers coming and going all times of the day and night. Rather than chance half-drunk ruffians catching them with a hoard of gold, Casey and Marsh had passed it by.

But now she and Dan had found it! She could hardly wait to throw open the boxes and run her fingers through the gold and jewels.

Suddenly, a blinding light flashed in her eyes.

"Police! Freeze!"

Nine

The sun was up and the birds were singing when the university police let them off at the Bronco. Dan's jaw was clamped shut and he looked mad enough to spit thunderbolts. He didn't even glance her way after they climbed into the cab.

"Dan—"

"Don't say a word. Not a word. Not now." He gave the key a smart turn and revved the engine. Holding the steering wheel in a white-knuckled grip, he sucked in a big breath before he pulled away from the curb.

He kept his eyes on the road as they drove up the boulevard, turned left on North Street, and headed south toward downtown. Once or twice Tess started to say something, but the formidable man hunched over the wheel didn't invite conversation. She was just as tired and just as humiliated as he was, but until he cooled off a bit, she'd bite her tongue and keep her mouth shut. She understood about discretion and valor.

When she saw his shoulders relax and the grooves in his face soften a bit, she decided to venture a comment. "Dan, I'm sorry about getting us carted off to the pokey for nothing. But how was I to know that the Old Stone Fort had been moved? I thought it had always been on the campus."

He didn't respond.

"I suppose I should have considered that it's quite a distance from downtown. Towns usually stay in the same place—even after a hundred years." She managed a sickly smile. "At least the police chief had a good sense of humor."

"Did you notice that before or after he said I have to pay damages for criminal mischief?"

"No," she snapped, growing tired of his hostile attitude, "I noticed it when he nearly split his sides laughing when you spouted off about Laffite's treasure map. What possessed you to tell him about my map?"

"The truth was better than that idiotic tale you invented about being on a scavenger hunt."

She stiffened her spine and tilted her nose. "It might have worked."

He made a rude sound.

Tess refused to be daunted any longer by his fractious behavior. "Why don't we check out the original site the policeman told us about?" she asked.

He slowly turned his head and looked at her as if she'd suggested that they defect to China.

Crossing her arms, she sniffed. "Well, it wouldn't hurt to look."

He heaved a big sigh and shook his head, but a few minutes later he pulled to a stop on the brick-paved main street. Businesses were not yet open and the district was almost deserted. They got out and crossed the intersection to read the brass plaque in front of a large building.

"Yep, it was here," Tess said looking up at the hulking red brick structure that covered half a block. "I wonder—"

"No!"

She raised her eyebrows. "No, what?"

"I'm not blowing up a bank, Tess. Not even for you."

She laughed and hooked her arm through his. Looking up at him with a puckish sparkle in her eyes, she pursed her lips. "Hmmm. I hadn't considered that, but—"

As he silenced her with a forefinger over her lips, a trace of amusement played around his mouth. "Don't even think it."

Smiling, she said; "I was just wondering if they found anything when the land was sold and the original fort was torn down in 1902. They must have excavated the area before they built here."

"We'll never know."

She laid her head against his shoulder and sighed. "We'll never know. And it looks like our last chance for my house and Pirate's Pleasure are kaput." Tears stung her eyes, and despite her efforts to keep them in check, one escaped and rolled down her cheek.

Dan hugged her close and wiped the tear away with his thumb. "Maybe not."

Her heart surged with new hope. "Do you think we could get some divers to find the stash under the lake? Or maybe we could rent one of those big earthmoving machines and search the place by the springs again."

"No, babe, I think finding any of Laffite's treasure

is a lost cause. Let's get some rest and head back to Galveston. We'll talk about options later."

"Are you still angry with me?"

He smiled and shook his head. "I wasn't really angry with you, love. I was frustrated and embarrassed."

They went back in their hotel room, cleaned up, and slipped into bed. Both were totally exhausted. Tess snuggled against Dan with her head on his shoulder and her hand across his chest.

"You never believed that we would find any treasure, did you?" She absently threaded her fingers through the fine curls along his breastbone, taking comfort from their silky texture and the warmth of the flesh beneath.

"No . . . and I should have talked you out of coming. I didn't want you to be disappointed."

"You couldn't have talked me out of it. I was so sure the gold was buried somewhere, just waiting for me to find it. I felt it deep down in here." She patted her chest. "It's strange, because when I get a feeling like that, I'm never wrong."

"This time you were."

She yawned. "I suppose. Sorry I dragged you along on my crazy adventure?"

He laughed and rubbed his cheek against her forehead. "I imagine, Tess Cameron, that life with you will be a series of adventures."

"I imagine," she breathed as her eyelids fluttered shut.

Tess awoke gradually, yawning and stretching. It took a moment for her to get her bearings. When she saw the familiar sampler on the wall across from the foot of her bed, she realized she was in her own room in Galveston. Aunt Olivia had told her that the sampler had belonged to Tess's mother, made for Anna's tenth birthday by her great-grandmother, Casey Prophet.

You may follow rainbows to find pots of gold, the stitching proclaimed, *but the real treasure of the family is in the foundation of our home.*

She threw aside the covers and got up grumbling, "That's all well and good for you, Granny, but *you* had a home. A hundred years of progress beat me out of my chance at the pot of gold."

In the bathroom, Tess turned on the shower and stripped off her nightgown. Her sleep had been fitful. Although she'd tried to be philosophical about not finding the treasure, especially around Dan, she'd been bitterly disappointed. For so long, all her fantasies had revolved around her house. No, not *her* house anymore. *The* house. Her option to buy would run out in two weeks. Perhaps she and Dan could find another, more affordable one, to restore. But it wouldn't be the same. That house had been meant for them, for their family. She knew it.

After her shower, she searched through her closet to find something to restore her spirits, but not even her favorite orange overalls and fuchsia camp shirt helped. She dawdled with her makeup, hating to go downstairs with the bad news. It had been late when they got home the night before, and everyone had been in bed. Now it was time to face Aunt Olivia and Aunt Martha with the fact that there would be no horse, no house. There was no treasure. Damn!

When her shoes were finally tied and her last excuse used up, she pasted a bright smile on her face and went downstairs. Dan and the entire crew were gathered around the dining table having breakfast. From the look on their faces when she walked in, she knew that Dan had already told them that their trip had been a total washout. She was grateful he'd spared her the task.

"Good morning," she said to the group, striding into the room on a ray of sunny laughter. "I guess Dan's told you that the bedraggled knights have returned without the Holy Grail. Even though we didn't find anything, we had a grand adventure. Some of it was a real hoot, wasn't it Dan? Did you tell them about our run-in with the law?"

A band of pain constricted Dan's heart when he looked up and saw Tess. Although no one would guess from her broad smile and jaunty step, he knew she was hurting. And he would have given his last dime to be able to soothe the hurt away. Tess was so used to giving to others, and people were so accustomed to taking from her that he suspected that no one ever considered that Tess had needs of her own. She was as strong and gutsy as any woman he'd ever known, but she needed someone to take care of her sometimes. She needed *him*.

Dan rose and smiled at her, hoping that the love and concern he felt shone in his face. "I was saving that tale for you." He helped her into her chair.

Ivan stood. "I make my best French toast just for you. Don't start the story until I get back." He strode from the room.

Tess glanced at the two older women. "I'm sorry Aunt Olivia, Aunt Martha. It looks like your plans for Pirate's Pleasure are out the window."

Olivia shrugged and gave a dismissing wave of her hand. "Easy come, easy go. Don't sweat it."

Martha reached across and patted Tess's hand. "Oh, pooh, Tess, what did two old ladies need with a racehorse anyway? If you want to know the truth, horses are really very messy, smelly creatures. Aren't they, Olivia?"

Olivia nodded. "Piles and piles of very smelly mess."

Hook's gold tooth gleamed as a grin split his face. He poured Tess a cup of coffee and passed it to her. "I want to hear about *your* brush with the law."

"Not till I get back!" Ivan shouted from the kitchen.

By the time breakfast was over, Tess and Dan had everyone laughing at the embroidered version of their exploits. Each tried to outdo the other as they related their quest.

"Police! Freeze!" Ivan boomed, then slapped the table as he guffawed. "I wish I could have seen the looks on your faces."

"Danny"—concern wrinkled Martha's brow as she leaned over to her grandson—"does this mean you'll have a record?"

He laughed. "I think I can still pass for a solid citizen, Gram." He glanced over at Tess, who looked like she had had all the phony joie de vivre she could handle for a while. "Tess," he said, rising, "next week is my sister Kathy's birthday. I thought I'd go shopping for something on the Strand, and I need some help picking out a proper gift. Would you come along?"

"Danny, I'd love—" Martha jumped and gave a little yelp. She glanced at Olivia, then pursed her lips into a tight pucker.

Hook's gold tooth flashed, and Ivan became acutely interested in his fingernails.

"Yes, Gram?"

Martha shot Olivia a haughty look and said, "I was just going to say that I'd love for you and Tess to pick out something for me to send Kathy as well."

"Let's go," Tess answered. "I'm in the mood for some shopping."

She jumped up, waved good-bye, and headed out the door with Dan in tow before anyone else could say a word. She was glad to escape for a while. Her disappointment would fade with time, someday she would be able to look back over their exploits and truly laugh, but just now the wounds were too fresh to keep pouring salt over them by talking about it and forcing laughter she didn't truly feel. For the rest of the day, she didn't even want to think about buried treasure.

They drove Buttercup to the Strand and parked on a side street.

"What kind of things does Kathy like?"

"What does every woman like? Clothes and jewelry. But she always complains that everything I buy for her is too conservative."

Tess grinned. "Nobody has ever accused me of that."

Dan laughed. "Why doesn't that surprise me?" He pulled a picture of Kathy from his wallet and handed it to Tess. "All of her sizes are on the back."

She studied the photograph of the pretty strawberry blond, who shared a more feminine version of Dan's features, then turned it over and glanced at her statistics. "I know just the thing. It's in the shop on the corner."

They got out and walked the half block to Morgan's. Once inside, she greeted the owner of the campy boutique and headed for a rack of silk separates. Flipping through the clothes for the proper sizes, she selected a gossamer-fine jacket of celery-colored silk, handpainted with dramatic coral lotus blossoms, and a matching camisole, pants, and skirt in solid celery.

"This is perfect for Kathy," she declared. "With her coloring, it will be fantastic. I'd love to have this outfit myself, but this shade makes me look like I'm recovering from a long bout with dengue fever." She thrust the garments at the proprietor. "Wrap them up, Pat. Birthday present."

She grabbed Dan's hand and steered him to a display of unusual costume jewelry. Scanning the table's contents, she picked up a pair of earrings that looked like fried eggs and held them to her ears. "What do you think?"

Dan looked pained.

She chortled. "Just checking. Pretty bad, huh?" She selected a necklace of hammered copper with an unusual starburst medallion and matching earrings. "For Kathy from your grandmother." Picking up a pair of paper-mâché watermelon slices, she threaded the hooks through her ears, turned to Dan and grinned. "For me from me. Like them?"

He smiled. "I like them. Strangely enough, on you they look perfect." He whispered in her ear, "Good enough to eat."

When they left the shop two hours later, their arms were piled high with packages. Besides the gifts for Kathy, Dan had insisted that she try on several outfits that caught her eye. He'd laughed at some, whistled appreciatively at others, and they'd bought most of them. Not once did he complain about spending time there.

After they had dumped their purchases in Buttercup, Tess grinned and kissed Dan on the cheek. "Nothing lifts my spirits like shopping for new clothes. You're a good sport, Friday. And because you are, I'm going to treat you to a tour that you'll love. Come on." She tugged at his hand and they took off at a swinging stride down the street.

"Where are we going?"

She pulled him into a souvenir shop. "You'll see. But first we need to be properly attired."

After much grumbling and giggling and laughing, they left the shop with gaudily plumed buccaneer hats on their heads and plastic sabers strapped to their sides. Strangely enough, nobody gave them a second glance.

Tess gave him a triumphant poke in the ribs with her elbow. "Told you," she said out of the side of her mouth. "This is Galveston. Everybody is a little crazy. It's allowed."

Hand in hand they walked to Water Street and down a few blocks to a row of warehouses backed up to the wharf.

"We're going to tour a warehouse?"

She laughed. "Just wait." She pulled him through a door in the musty, cavernous building and waved to an old man sitting at a table reading a newspaper. "Hi, Gus. We're going to take a look at *Proud Beauty*. How's she coming along?"

The old man touched the bill of his seaman's cap. "Fine. Just fine. Mr. Marshall's ordered the sails from a place in Maine. Won't be many more weeks before we'll be rigging her to take out."

From the rear of the warehouse, they walked out on a pier and Tess gave an exaggerated sweep of her hand, pointing to the large sailing vessel berthed there. Perfectly restored, her tall masts awaiting their square-rigged sails, she sat anchored in the water. "Meet *Proud Beauty.*"

Hands on his hips, Dan looked the ship over from the bow's figurehead to the stern rail, from the tip of the mainmast to the freshly painted wooden hull. "She is a beauty. Who owns her?"

"A friend of Dr. Ed's from Houston. He's been working on restorations for three years. Even though he could well afford to have it all done for him, he enjoys helping the work crews himself. Come on," she said, kicking off her shoes, and motioning for him to do the same, "let's go aboard."

"Are you sure the owner won't mind?"

"Positive. We let him use the warehouse and pier for free." She bent to roll up the legs of her orange overalls.

"We?" He rolled up his pant legs in imitation of Tess.

"Aunt Olivia and me." She grinned. "This was the other piece of property Laffite willed Violet." Running toward the gangplank, she yelled over her shoulder. "Last one on deck is a lily-livered coward."

Grinning, he took off after her. She led him below and they toured the hold, the galley, and the quarters for officers and crew. Dan kissed her outside the captain's cabin, but Tess laughed and twisted away. "Cease, you blackguard or be keelhauled! No man kisses the pirate queen!"

Scurrying up the companionway, she ran to the wheel and grabbed it with both hands. Feet spread apart, she closed her eyes and listened to the cry of seagulls overhead and the water licking against the hull. A breeze had kicked up. It caressed her cheeks with damp sea air, carried green ocean smells and the scents of wax and wet new wood. She held her face to the play of the wind and imagined canvas flapping overhead as the ship bobbed gently beneath her bare feet. How grand it must have been to have sailed the seas in Laffite's day. She could almost hear the roar of cannons and the clash of cutlasses.

Dan's arms clamped around her waist. "Gotcha, my pretty," he growled in her ear.

Squealing with laughter, she slipped from his grasp. Two steps away, she wheeled, drew her plastic saber, and shouted, "Back, back, you scurvy sea-dog! Back or you die."

For a moment, the breeze ruffling the red plume on his hat was his only movement. Then his eyes narrowed, his lip drew into a lascivious sneer, and he reached for his sword.

"Give over, my bloodthirsty vixen," he growled in his deepest voice. "You're mine."

She thrust her nose in the air and exclaimed in a falsetto, "No, never."

Uttering a theatrical, villainous laugh, he grabbed her and threw her over his shoulder like a sack of coffee beans. "We'll see about that." Her hat went tumbling across the deck as he strode to the companionway.

"My hat!" she squealed as its yellow plume disappeared over the side.

"I'll buy you a thousand hats after I have my way with you."

She wiggled and giggled and beat on his back with her fists. "Unhand me, you bloody cutthroat."

He smacked her on the bottom. "Quiet, wench, you're no lightweight."

He carried her down the narrow steps to the captain's quarters and dropped her on the bunk. Her eyes widened as she looked up at him. "Surely you wouldn't ravish an innocent maiden."

Eyebrow quirked at a wicked angle and one corner of his mouth raised in a satyric smirk, his gaze burned a path from toe to nose. "No."

She heaved a sigh. "Oh, shoot." She started to rise.

Laughing, he captured her in his arms and fell onto the bunk with her. "But I plan to ravish *you.*" Soft blue-gray eyes, the same shade as the shirt he wore, scanned her face. His hand pushed her tousled hair. "Mind?"

"Do your duty, mate." She took off his hat and tossed it aside.

He lowered his lips to hers and tasted and teased and tormented with the tip of his tongue until her arms slipped around his neck and pulled him into a kiss that curled her toes.

"Oh, God," Dan whispered, fumbling with the clasps of her overall bib. "Woman, you set me on fire."

Slowly, he pulled the garment down over her hips and along her legs to her ankles, his eyes feasting on her as he went. She kicked her feet free, and with a roguish chuckle that made her breath catch, he pitched the orange wad over his shoulder.

His hands slid up the outside of her legs, along the curve of her hips, and under her fuchsia shirt to cup her breasts as he sought her mouth.

Amid urgent kisses, they stripped one another, tossing clothes aside until they lay bare on the captain's bunk.

Dan's tongue circled her navel, then dipped into the shallow recess. She moaned and threaded her fingers through his thick mane of hair as he kissed a wet, winding trail over her belly and up to the underside of her breast. He licked and laved and kissed his way around one soft mound until his lips closed over its hardened peak. She drew in a quiet scream as he nibbled and sucked at the sensitive tip while his hand slipped between her thighs.

Her movements grew fevered and frantic as his mouth and fingers worked fiery magic on her flesh. She reached for him but he twisted away.

"Not yet, me pretty, I'm not done with my tormenting."

And he wasn't.

"Dannn!" she squeaked as his mouth went lower.

By the time he knelt between her legs, she was a mindless bundle of sensation—raw, exposed, arching, aching for release. He hooked his arms under her knees and grinned down at her, his nostrils flared, his need as evident and great as hers.

"You want me, my comely wench?"

She whimpered and nodded.

"You got me."

He raised her up and plunged deeply. He drew back and thrust again. A hurricane of desire swirled over her and swept her up in its tempest. Flinging herself forward, she rocked him to his back and sat astride him. His arms snaked out to catch her waist.

She smiled down at the ecstasy that drew the cords of his neck and opened his mouth in a soundless groan. She rotated her hips and the sound became audible.

Rotating her hips again and again, they strained

against one another—giving pleasure, taking pleasure, until the hurricane increased in intensity and roared over them with a fury that ripped release from their bodies.

Tess slumped forward against his damp chest and he held her tight. "Tess, my Tess. How could I ever live without you?"

They lay still until their ragged breathing had calmed and their heartbeats slowed. "I love you, Dan. I love you so much."

He rubbed his chin across the top of her head. "And I love you. Tess, will you marry me?"

"Of course," she said, snuggling and settling closer in the comfort of his arms. "I always intended to."

The deep rumble of his laughter vibrated against her cheek and the hand splayed across his chest. "Just like that? Love, you never cease to amaze me."

She smiled. Life with Dan would be so wonderful. Even though they couldn't have the house she'd wanted for their family, they would find another to restore. It would be so beautiful that soon everyone in Galveston would know what a fine restoration architect Dan was. Clients would be beating the door down with projects for him. He'd have his dream, and she—well, having him, knowing that he was happy and healthy, and sharing his love was worth more than any house in the world.

The gentle sway of the ship lulled them and they closed their eyes.

"Ahoy, there!" At the sound, their eyes flew open. They could hear footsteps on the deck above.

"Oh, my God! It's Gus!" Tess jumped up and they began scrambling for their clothes. Dan pulled on his briefs and his pants and grabbed his shirt while she fumbled with the hooks on her bra. "Do something," she hissed at him.

"Ahoy, there!" Dan called out the door as he yanked his shirt over his head.

"Got a man here to deliver some fittings for the galley," came the voice from above.

"Stall him," she whispered. Dan grinned and went up the companionway as she grabbed up her shirt and overalls. Hurrying as fast as she could, she dressed and, after finger-combing her hair, stuck the red-plumed buccaneer hat on her head. She quickly straightened the bunk, picked up Dan's sword, took a deep breath, and went topside.

They said their good-byes to Gus, who grinned the whole time, and went down the gangplank to the warehouse.

"I couldn't find my panties," Tess said out of the side of her mouth.

"They're in my pocket."

"How did they get there?"

"They were tangled in my shirt."

She rolled her eyes. "I could die of embarrassment."

"Why? I don't think Gus suspected anything."

"No?" She gave a little snort. "Your shirt is inside out."

They hitched a ride back to the car in Amos's carriage and stopped by a service station to make a few repairs to their appearance. They ate a late lunch in an old dining car on the tracks at the railroad museum and spent the rest of the afternoon walking barefoot on the beach.

They held hands and laughed over nothing. They filled their pockets with shells, and watched children building sandcastles. They ate strawberry snow cones while they watched two young men fly elaborate triple- and quadruple-rowed kites through intricate maneuvers. They basked in the sunshine and in their love for one another. When the air began to chill, they turned and walked to the car.

"Feeling better about the treasure?" Dan asked as he wiped the sand off her feet before they got into Buttercup.

She shrugged. "I suppose. I haven't thought about it very much." When she closed the car door, a bittersweet vision of her house flashed into her mind. "Would you do me a favor?"

"Anything." He smiled and reached across to stroke her cheek with the back of his hand.

"Would you go with me to say good-bye to the house?"

Dan opened his mouth to speak, then stopped. "Sure."

Each lost in quiet thoughts and plans, they drove to the corner where the strange, small palace with the rusticated stucco walls sat amid creeping vines and overgrown shrubs. Tess got out, leaned against the iron fence, and looked up at the sculpted torch on the tower and at the nine gables along the gray slate roof. It looked so forlorn that she wanted to weep.

Indeed she must have, for Dan gathered her in his arms and said, "Oh, babe, don't cry. If you want that house so much, we'll buy it. It may not be practical with us living in Pittsburgh, but what the hell. We can come down for a weekend now and then and a few days during the summer."

A sharp stab of pain gouged deep into her heart. Her mouth went dry and a vacuum of shock sucked all the air from her lungs. Panic gripped her stomach. Eyes wide and wild, she drew back and stared at him. Surely she'd misunderstood.

"What are you talking about?"

"I'll buy you the house for a wedding present." He smiled. "I can afford it."

"Forget the house!" Her fingers dug into his upper arms as she searched his face. "What did you say about living in Pittsburgh?"

His smile faded. "Sweetheart, I know you're not fond of cities," he said, his tone gentle and appeasing, "but that's where my work is."

"Your work?"

"Friday Elevators, remember?"

"Friday Elevators?" Her voice was a shrill squeak. "You can't go back there! You hate it! It almost killed you!"

"Honey, I'm okay now, and the company is my responsibility. I can't let Kathy continue to shoulder a burden that's rightfully mine."

"You're going to stay here in Galveston and be an architect. Just as you always dreamed." She ground the words out and shook him as if to convince him with the force of her will.

He pulled her against his chest. "Oh, love, I wish I could, but that was just a fleeting fantasy. The reality is that I'm head of the family, and I belong as president of the company. A lot of people depend on me."

"No!" She jerked away. "I won't let you go back to the way you were. I won't let you kill yourself. You've been happy here."

"Tess, please try to understand. I have to return to Pittsburgh soon. It's been a wonderful vacation, but

I've stayed away from my business longer than I ever intended. I can't expect Kathy to continue doing my job. She'll buckle under the strain. Let's get married right away, and you can come back with me." He lifted her chin and smiled at her. "You can keep me from eating french fries and make sure I take my medicine."

"You stubborn idiot!" She beat on his chest with her fists as tears streamed down her face. "I won't go with you. I won't move to Pittsburgh!"

He grabbed her wrists. "Tess, be reasonable. I have to go back."

Regret, as deep and aching as any pain she'd ever felt, hovered over her heart like a dark, gathering storm, and its clouds painted her soul an empty, ominous black. "I won't help you commit suicide. If you go, Daniel Friday, you'll go alone."

Ten

The room was dark. It matched his mood. Dan sat in an easy chair in his posh high-rise apartment in Pittsburgh's Mount Washington district. He stared out the window at the lights of the city below, the glow of Three Rivers Stadium, and the shadowy trees in the park where the winding rivers met. He'd lived here all his life and the sights should have comforted him, made him feel at home. But strangely enough, he felt like an alien in the familiar surroundings. And he'd never been as lonely in his life.

For three days, he'd stayed in Galveston and begged and wheedled and promised Tess the moon if she'd come back with him. With her at his side, even running the company would have been bearable. But she'd refused to budge.

Exasperated, he'd left. He'd give her a few days, then he'd call. Perhaps when she'd had time to think things over, she'd come around. They loved each other, and people who loved enough could work things out if they were determined. And he was.

Tomorrow morning, he'd report to his office in the plant on the Monongahela River and take over from Kathy. Already his stomach burned at the thought.

He took a sip of the eggnog Ivan had sent along in a thermos. He ought to fix something for dinner—Ivan had sent a detailed menu as well, and Gram had called ahead to be sure Kathy had stocked his refrigerator and pantry—but he wasn't hungry. Only Tess's face filled his mind.

Lord, he missed her.

"No, Dan, I haven't changed my mind. I'm sorry." Tess gripped the phone tightly and squeezed her eyes shut to hold back the tears. "I'm sorry," she whispered. "I can't. I won't." Before her voice broke, she gently replaced the receiver on the hook and fell back across her bed.

It was the second time in the week since Dan had been gone that he'd called. Seven days. Seven days of misery. Several times she'd been tempted to defy her good judgment and fly to Pittsburgh. Once she'd even gone as far as dragging her suitcase out of the closet, but she'd forced herself to put it back.

If she caved in, she'd be with Dan and they might be happy for a while, but she would hate being caught up in the corporate rat race again. If she went, sooner or later Dan would slip back into his old ways. She could envision the pattern. It would be this emergency or that, a few extra hours here and there, and before he realized it, he'd be a workaholic with a bleeding ulcer again. Their relationship would become more and more strained until love turned to resentment and there would be nothing left. Didn't he know what going back to his old habits would do to him? Did he have some kind of unconscious death wish?

A part of her believed that perhaps Dan loved her enough to forget that damned elevator company. Any day now, he'd discover that he was not indispensable to a stupid business that he despised, that his family would be happier if he'd follow his own dream. But he was stuffed to the gills with integrity. She sighed. The same strength of character that was making him so stubborn was one of the many things that attracted her to him. If he were any different, he wouldn't be the same man she loved.

Damn! She grabbed a pillow and flung it across the room. It hit the sampler and set it swinging on its hook. The embroidered words seemed to mock her. It seemed as if the fates were conspiring against her and snickering about it.

"But I didn't get my home, Granny Prophet!" she shouted at the taunting axiom. "The treasure is gone and the man I love is determined to become a martyr!"

She got in bed, curled into a fetal position, and pulled the covers over her head. She might as well accept the fact that she and Dan were finished. He'd made his decision, and she'd made hers. He wouldn't change his mind, and she couldn't. It was a deadlock. And she was wretchedly bitter and angry and miserable, miserable, miserable.

If she didn't stop wallowing in her misery soon, forget about a life with Dan, and get on with the one she had, she'd go mad. She had friends and family and businesses to occupy her time and energy. She'd survived worse things—though, at the moment, she couldn't recall what.

Maybe, she decided as she got up to get her pillow,

she'd look into the feasibility of hiring a team of divers to search Lake Livingston. Maybe launching herself into a new project would keep her mind off Dan. Her option to buy the house still had a few days to go. Maybe she could still salvage a remnant of her dream. Maybe.

She picked up Casey's journal and the folder of papers that the clerk in Livingston had copied for them. She glanced through the sheaf of plats and deeds and tax roll information, but her perusal was only halfhearted, and she laid them on her night-stand to wait for another time.

Twisting and turning, she punched her pillow a dozen times before she finally fell into a restless sleep.

Her dreams were filled with rainbows and pots of gold chasing her. She tried to elude them, to run and hide, but each time they found her hiding place and forced her to run again until they chased her into the basement. Rainbows like giant ribbons of cellophane tape swooped around her, trying to stick to her head, while pots dive-bombed her like frantic bats and dumped showers of gold coins with every pass. Covering her head with her arms, she ran round and round, sinking deeper into the dirt as she tried to escape. When she was up to her knees and couldn't move, the floor caved in and an eleva-tor zipped her to the deck of a Spanish galleon. The deck was piled high with gold and gemstones that hurt her bare feet to walk across them.

At the helm of the ship stood a woman who looked like Casey Prophet, in the portrait down the hall. A red-plumed buccaneer's hat topped her flowing hair and her long dress billowed behind her like a rainbow-colored sail. Long strings of jewels around her neck sparkled as she threw back her head and laughed. "The Bible!" she shouted over the howling wind and pounding waves. "Remember your Bible verses!"

Heart racing, Tess's eyes flew open and she sat straight up in bed. Relieved to find that she'd been dreaming, she lay back down and took deep breaths, waiting for her heartbeat to slow.

Remembering the bizarre happenings that had seemed so real, she shook her head. "How weird."

Even though her day was busy, helping Becky at the Mermaid in the morning and filling in for Nancy at the Sea Song in the afternoon, the dream continued to bother her. It popped into her mind at the strangest times.

After dinner that evening, Tess wandered into the second floor sitting room where the two older women were playing cribbage. "Aunt Olivia," she asked, sitting on the arm of her aunt's chair, "do you remember much about your grandmother Casey?"

"Oh, my, yes. After Poppa died, we moved back here with her and Grandpa Marsh. Octavia and I were only six, and she practically raised us. She was a gas."

"I remember her, too," Martha said, laying down her cards. "I always loved to visit Olivia and Octavia because their grandmother was such fun. She had a yellow Dusenberg roadster that she would load a bunch of us kids in, and we'd go zipping around town, singing at the tops of our lungs. What ever happened to that roadster, Olivia?"

"As I recall, she drove it off a pier one New Year's Eve. Jumped before it hit the water. She said the brakes went out, but Grandpa was mad as a hornet.

He gave her holy hell. Said one of these days she was going to kill herself with her crazy antics." She laughed. "Grandma lived to be ninety-three."

"They used to give such wonderful parties. And how she loved scavenger hunts and treasure hunts. Why, I remember one—it must have been when you and Octavia were sixteen—that she had us chasing all over the island for clues. Wade Dorset caught his pants on fire getting one out of the hotel chimney."

Before the two launched into any more reminiscences, Tess asked her aunt, "Do you remember something about Grandma Casey and Bible verses?"

"Do I ever!" Olivia put her hand on her chest and rolled her eyes. "There were twenty-seven of them. Momma had to learn them, and Octavia and I had to learn them. And we had to solemnly promise to teach them to our children. I remember Grandma teaching them to your mother, too, from the time she was ten. At least once a year until she died, she would call each of us in and have us recite. If we complained, she would scowl at us, pat her Bible, and say, 'The secret of this family's blessing is in this book. Never forget it.' I think one of the reasons I stayed away from home so much after I graduated from college was to get out of reciting those blasted verses."

An elusive childhood memory flitted through Tess's mind. "Did Grandma Octavia teach them to me?"

Olivia laughed. "She tried to, but you always got them mixed up and cried. I think she finally gave up."

"Do you remember them?"

"It's been over thirty years since Grandma died. I'm not sure I can recite them anymore." Cocking her head and fluttering her long eyelashes, Olivia said, "I believe the first one was Proverbs 8:21 and the next, Proverbs 8:33. And let me see, I think the next one was in Psalms. Or was it Ecclesiastes? Maybe it was Luke. Oh, dear, Tess, it's been too long. What made you think of Grandma's verses?"

"Something I dreamed about. I'm going up to read for a while. If I don't see you in the morning before you leave, have a safe and fun trip." She kissed her aunt's cheek.

"Are you sure you won't come and spend a few days at the farm with us?" Olivia asked. "You always enjoy the races, too."

"Not this time, thanks." She bent to kiss Martha good night.

Martha captured her hand. "Tess, I'm so sorry things didn't work out with Danny. I was hoping—"

"I know, Aunt Martha." Tess patted the blue-veined hand. "It's okay." Swallowing the lump in her throat, she managed a smile. She'd hadn't told either of the women how far her relationship with Dan had progressed. There hadn't been time to announce their engagement before it was broken. Now it was just as well. "Good night."

In her room, Tess propped up in her bed and picked up Casey's journal of adventures in searching for treasure along the "rainbow trail" marked by the multicolored stones on the Bible case. She read the whole thing through again. It ended with finding the four chests near San Augustine in east Texas.

Laying the book aside, she leaned back against the pillows and stared at the sampler. Knowing what she did about Grandma Prophet, it didn't make sense that Casey would leave a fortune buried in the ground when, even a hundred years ago, civilization was encroaching on the hiding places.

Suddenly, a thought popped into her head and she grabbed the folder of papers from the Livingston court house. She searched through them until she saw a familiar name. She froze.

There it was.

She threw back her head and laughed. "Granny, you sly dog!"

In 1889, Acacia Prophet had purchased Nathan Power's farm for fifteen hundred dollars. She sold it a few years later for less than half what she paid for it. Tess giggled. Some people probably thought that Grandma Casey was a poor businesswoman.

Well, so much for the idea of divers. Casey had probably dug up the other treasure as well.

Still smiling at the bittersweet loss of her last hope for her house, she looked at the sampler which had belonged to Anna. It was the only personal thing of her mother's that she owned, and, for as long as she could remember, it had hung in the same spot in her room in Galveston. She glanced to the rocker in the corner and recalled lovely memories of Grandma Octavia sitting in the chair, with Tess in her lap, telling her stories of all the wonderful women in their family. Not one of the ladies had ever been conformists. They'd all been free-spirited, fun-loving, ready to try anything, and devil take the hindmost. For some reason, only girls had been born in the family, never a single boy.

She got up, placed the journal and the papers on her desk, and went to draw her bath.

Heart pounding and her breath coming in short gasps, Tess struggled to wake from her dream. Casey Prophet's laughter still echoed in her ears, and she could hear her shout over the wind and water, "Remember your Bible verses!"

Her eyes opened and she jerked upright. It was the same dream! Every bit of it was an exact repeat of the night before. It was so real that she felt her hair to see if there were rainbow tapes stuck on her head.

Why had she had the dream again?

She got up, went to the bathroom, and washed her face. The whole time she brushed her teeth, the words came over and over in her mind. *Remember your Bible verses.*

Pulling on red knit shorts and a matching T-shirt, she went downstairs. Although the house was empty and quiet, the delicious aroma of coffee wafted through the rooms. The four had already left for the farm in Louisiana, but the red light on the pot was on.

"Bless you, dear Ivan," she said, pouring a mug and taking a sip.

Leaning against the counter, she took another swallow. *Remember your Bible verses.* The admonition went round and round in her head, playing mental hide-and-seek with a vague, elusive memory of something Grandma Octavia had told her when she was a little girl. What was it?

She filled her mug again and took it upstairs with her. In her room, she went to her desk and found the little white Bible her grandmother had given her when she was eight. Opening it, she read the writing on the fly page.

Our family has been blessed with both love and material things. If ever you or your chil-

dren have a need, tell them of our rainbow and our secret verses.

Suddenly, the memory popped up of Grandma Octavia rocking her and saying, "Shhhh, Tess, don't cry. We'll write them down and put them in a secret place. And one day, when you have a little girl, you can tell her about it."

The secret place.

She walked to the sampler and took it off the wall. Glued to the backing was an envelope, yellowed with age. Inside was a card which listed twenty-seven verses. The first two were Proverbs, just as Aunt Olivia had remembered. What was so special and secret about those verses? Were they intended as some kind of message? She started to pick up her white Bible to look them up, but something made her pause.

No, not this one. The other one. She laid the card on her desk.

Her heart thudded against her ribs as she went to Olivia's sitting room to retrieve Violet's Bible from the old trunk. The familiar smell of camphor touched her nose as she opened the curved top. She picked up the stone-studded case and closed the trunk lid. Hugging the wooden box to her, she resisted the urge to run back to her room. Instead she walked very slowly and reminded herself to breathe normally.

She placed the case on her bed and ran her fingers over the meandering trail of stones on the front. The first one was red; the second, orange; then, yellow, green, blue, indigo, and violet. The colors of the rainbow.

As if in slow motion, she took the Bible from its case and carried it to her desk. Sitting down, she pulled a pen and pad from a drawer and propped the card against the crown of a red-plumed buccaneer's hat.

She sucked in a deep breath and opened the book to the eighth chapter of Proverbs. The words of verse twenty-one were underlined.

That I may cause those that love me to inherit substance; and I will fill their treasures.

She wrote it on the pad and turned to the thirty-third verse of the same chapter. It, too, was underlined.

Hear instruction, and be wise, and refuse it not.

Okay, she thought, the words were nice but was there a message here? The next was a selection from Ecclesiastes.

I gathered me also silver and gold, and the peculiar treasure of kings and of the provinces. . . .

Her heart began to flutter, and a sheen of perspiration broke out on her upper lip. Was Casey talking about recovering the treasure? She quickly wrote down the next five, which were only a few words underlined from passages in Psalms, Acts, 2 Samuel, and Mark.

From power . . . the church in the wilderness . . . rock . . . fortress . . . treasure . . . I will shew you . . .

Her heart started pounding in earnest and her hands shook as a slow grin spread across her face. *From power* was Nathan Power's farm; *the church in the wilderness* was the place outside Lufkin where the church had once been near the springs; the *rock fortress* was the Old Stone Fort. Looking up, she squeezed her fists in a gesture of excitement. Grandma Prophet had gathered up the treasure in all the other places. No wonder she and Dan couldn't find it.

"But what did you do with all of it, Granny? Show me, show me!" She checked the next several verses, which had a word here and a phrase there under- lined, and wrote them down.

. . . a bride . . . built a house . . . laid the foun- dation . . .

Violet?

. . . the flood rose . . . shaken of a mighty wind . . . So we built the wall . . .

"You're talking about the great hurricane and build- ing the seawall."

. . . out of great tribulation . . . island . . . moved . . . my house . . . filled . . .

The grade-raising of Galveston when the yard and the basement were filled in! Tess wiped the perspi- ration off her lip with the back of her hand, took another deep breath, and went back to her task.

. . . in the earth, hid . . . money . . . earth on top . . . the earth is full of thy riches . . .

"Yippeee!" Tess screamed and threw her pen in the air. "The treasure is in the basement! My, God, all these years, we've been sitting on a fortune. Where in the basement, Granny?" She retrieved her pen from where it had rolled under the bed and sat down to decipher the last eight verses.

When she'd finished, she held up her pad and read the last words aloud. "Seek, and ye shall find under the place where she hath also furnished her table, a place for the gold. Find the blessing in thine house. It shall be an inheritance for what things ye have need of."

Tossing down her pen, she closed her eyes and dropped her head back. For almost a hundred years, an unbelievable treasure had been buried in the basement under the dining table. She looked at the sampler Grandma Prophet had stitched for Tess's mother, Anna, and laughed. Now, the words made sense.

You may follow rainbows to find pots of gold, but the real treasure of the family is in the foundation of our home.

All she had to do was go downstairs and dig it up. There would be riches enough to buy her house and a whole string of racehorses for Aunt Olivia and Aunt Martha. She could probably buy Friday Elevators and close the damned place down if she'd a mind to. The thought was tempting.

Her only regret was that there was no one around to share in her good fortune. Not Aunt Olivia. Not Dan.

She sighed. And shrugged. Oh, well. She wasn't going to let any sad thoughts spoil her moment of triumph. She'd found the treasure. She'd finally found it!

And she was going to go downstairs and dig it up and laugh while she ran her fingers through every last bit of it.

It was as dark and musty as a tomb down there. It was a tomb of sorts. Maybe not as rich as King Tut's, but near enough for her, she thought as she held Hook's mechanic's light high. She'd tried a flashlight, but the darkness had swallowed up the pitiful beam. So she'd gone to the garage and found the brighter light. The long extension cord trailed behind her like a tail as she made her way to the spot she estimated to be directly under the dining table.

The ceiling of the basement was so low—or rather, the floor was so high—that Tess practically had to duck-walk or scoot on her knees to get around in some places. She swiped away a cobweb and sneezed at the dust it stirred.

She looped the lamp cord around a nail in a board overhead. It was probably the same nail Casey and Marsh had used to hang their lantern when they buried their treasure. Or did they have electricity then? She shrugged. No matter.

When the light was secure, she picked up the short-handled entrenching tool she'd found in the garage and knocked away more cobwebs. She sneezed again. Wiping her nose on her shirt sleeve, she began to dig. In only a few turns of the shovel, she hit metal.

"Tess!" a deep voice called out.

She froze. Who was out there? Had she locked the door? She couldn't remember.

"Tess! Where are you?"

Dan! It was Dan! Startled, she raised up, banged her head on a rafter, and let out a yelp. "I'm down here," she yelled. Hunched over to keep from bumping her head again, she started for the steps.

"Where?"

"Down here. In the basement. I'm coming."

When she got to the abbreviated stairway, she looked up to see Dan standing in the door. He was dressed in a business suit, complete with conservative tie. He frowned. "What in the hell are you doing down there? You're filthy."

Trying to make herself presentable, she swiped her hands over her hair and her clothes, but she only succeeded in raising a dust cloud and smearing spiderwebs on her hands.

"What in the hell are you doing in Galveston? I thought you were in Pittsburgh playing president of Friday Elevators."

He grinned. "I discovered it was no fun without you."

Her heart did a back-flip and her eyes widened. "Do you mean . . . ?"

He laughed. "I'm here for good. Know anybody who needs a good architect?"

Tess ran up the steps and hurled herself into his arms. "Oh, boy, do I!"

He swung her around, and they kissed and laughed and hugged and kissed again. "Oh, God, how I missed you, babe," he said, holding her close. "I don't think I've laughed once in the time I've been gone. My ulcer started acting up the first day I went to the office, and I was miserable without you. Kathy had done a great job as president while I was gone. I think everybody was sorry to see me come back. And she loves it. Can you imagine that? She actually enjoys being president."

Tess laughed and kissed him again. "There's no accounting for taste. Did she boot you out again?"

"No, when she saw me moping around and acting like a bear with everyone who crossed my path, she insisted that we have a heart-to-heart talk. For the first time we were honest with each other. I admitted that I hated the job and only continued with it out of a sense of obligation to the family and to protect her. She admitted that she's been dying to take over for a long time, especially after she saw me struggling through the past year or two, but she didn't want to hurt my pride by telling me. That sly sister of mine sent me to Galveston hoping Gram could talk me into retiring from the presidency."

"I think I'm going to like Kathy."

He grinned. "I think she's going to like you, too. By the way, she loved the gifts from Gram and me that you selected." His hand cupped the side of her neck and his thumb traced the line of her jaw in a tender, familiar gesture. "I don't want us ever to be apart again, love. Will you marry me as soon as possible?"

She gave a saucy grin. "I always intended to."

"I can scrape up enough to buy the house for you, and we can take our time restoring it."

She threw back her head and gave a low, throaty laugh. "Right now I have a surprise for you. Take off your coat and tie."

With a wicked gleam in his eye, Dan quirked an eyebrow. "You got it, babe." Before she could say a word, he shed his coat, dropped it on the floor, and yanked off his tie.

"Not for *that*." She gave him a playful swat. "That comes later. Right now I have a surprise for you." Grabbing him by the hand, she pulled him toward the steps. "Watch your head. There's not room to stand up down here."

"Where are we going?"

"We're going to dig for treasure."

Dan groaned. "Oh, no, not again."

"You just wait. This time I know absolutely, positively, without a single, solitary doubt, where the loot is buried."

"Where have I heard that before?"

With a little bob of her head, she gave a smug grin and offered him the shovel. "But that was before I knew about Granny Casey's Bible verses." With both of them kneeling in the basement fill dirt, he sighed, gave her an indulgent smile, and reached for the short-handled tool. She pulled it back, narrowed her eyes, and said, "You're not one of those macho types who would be intimidated by a rich wife, are you?"

Amusement lifted one corner of his mouth. "I think my ego can take it."

"Good, because we're about to be very, very rich. Dig."

He dug.

In a few minutes, the earth was cleared from a metal chest, dark and crusted with age. They looked at one another. "Open it, sweetheart," he said, sitting back on his heels.

Closing her eyes, she took a deep breath. Her heart was in her throat and her hands were shaking as she reached for the latch. She lifted it and slowly opened the lid. Some sort of fabric lay over the top. When she reached to pull it aside, it disintegrated in her hands.

Through the rotten remnants, something flashed in the light, and she brushed the scraps aside. Her eyes grew wide, and she sucked in a gasp. "Oh, Dannnn," she whispered.

"My . . . God."

The chest was brimming full of gold and silver bars, hundreds of Spanish gold coins, and all kinds of precious gems both mounted and loose.

Dan picked up a gold tiara, studded with pearls and rubies the size of quarters. He placed it on Tess's head and smiled. "It matches your outfit, my love." He clasped a necklace of similar design around her neck.

She looked down at the heavy piece, squealed, and

threw her arms around him. "Oh, Dan, we found it! We're rich!"

Laughing and crying and crazy with joy, she planted scores of smacking kisses all over his face. So exuberant were her kisses that they fell backward in the dirt with Tess sprawled across him. He held her and hooted with laughter.

When the shock wore off, she sobered and said, "Dan, this is only one. There are others." Her eyes flashed and her voice was full of wonder.

They started digging again. In a little more than two hours, they had unearthed twelve metal boxes, each filled with treasure.

Tess reached down, scooped a mound of gold coins up in her hand, and let them trickle through her fingers. "How much do you think is here?"

Dan sat down on one of the chests and wiped his face on the sleeve of his white dress shirt. He shook his head in amazement. "I have no idea."

"Do you think one chestful would be worth a million dollars?"

"I suspect that's a conservative estimate."

She was quiet for a moment, then said, "Jean Laffite provided well for his descendants. And Casey and Marsh Prophet made sure that it would be safe for coming generations. Why don't we keep out one for us and one for Aunt Olivia? The rest we can cover back up to leave for our children and our grandchildren."

He looked pained. "Right now?"

Sitting in the dirt beside him, covered with grime, with cobwebs in her hair and tiara slightly askew, Tess laughed and laid her head against his thigh. "Tomorrow will be soon enough. Let's go upstairs and take a bath. After all that work, I'm sure you're very tired and need to rest."

Raising one eyebrow in that deliciously wicked way of his, he said, "I'm not *that* tired."

Pursing her lips to keep from laughing, she said, "I see." She leaned close to him and gave him her most provocative smile. "Did I tell you that everybody is in Louisiana? We have the house all to ourselves for three whole days."

Epilogue

Over the bateau neckline of a long hostess gown, deep crimson and made of the softest velvet, Tess wore a heavy gold necklace, encrusted with pearls and bloodred rubies as big as quarters. They sat snuggled together on the huge, poofy couch covered in oyster suede and watched the firelight flicker in the Italian marble fireplace. Above the mantle hung Hook's painting of the blue water nymph with Tess's face. The colors matched the blue watered silk on the walls.

The smells of burning oak and fresh paint and wax mingled with those of warm cinnamon and nutmeg. A fragrance of potpourri and baby powder wafted through the high-ceilinged house as well.

A crystal bowl filled with pine and holly sat on the massive coffee table beside a wooden Bible case studded with a meandering trail of rainbow-colored stones. A magnificent Persian rug covered the polished oak floors.

"It's taken a long time, but at last it's all finished,"

Dan said, nuzzling the side of her neck. "Happy with it?"

"Very. I've never been happier in my life," Tess said, lifting her chin to give her husband better access to the spot where his tongue was doing delicious things. "I have everything any woman could ever want. You?"

"Very. And you were right. I have more clients now than I can handle."

In the corner stood a tall spruce, covered with gold balls and angels and great swags of gold and crystal beads. Three hundred twinkling lights reflected off the gleaming brass samovar on the long table next to it. Under the tree were great piles of gaily wrapped Christmas presents.

"Why don't you and I go upstairs?" he whispered.

"Can't." She sighed. "Hook went to pick up Kathy at the airport, and they should be here any minute. Aunt Olivia and Gram and Ivan said they'd be here for dinner at six. It's almost that now."

"What are we having for dinner?"

"I don't now. Ivan's bringing everything. He said it would be a traditional Bulgarian American Christmas Eve feast, whatever that means." She gave a deep, throaty laugh.

The sparkle in her eyes worked the same magic on him that it had when he'd first seen her. "How I love you, Tess."

She kissed the little freckle on the side of his mouth. "And I love you. Now and always, Friday."

The doorbell chimed.

"Up!" came a voice from the playpen at the end of the couch.

"Up!" came another.

Dan and Tess looked at one another. "I think the

twins are ready to play," she said. "The whole bunch is going to spoil the girls rotten. And you-know-who is the worst. I'll get Casey. You get Marsha."

They each picked up a small imp in identical green coveralls with identical red curls. Four new teeth peeked out from behind each twin's babyish version of their mother's million-kilowatt smile.

"Hook," said Casey, pointing one tiny, wet finger toward the door.

"Hook," echoed Marsha, kicking her feet against her father's hip.

"How do they know?" asked Dan.

Tess shrugged. "Beats me." She laughed and went to open the door.

Author's Note

Three of the houses mentioned in my story are loosely based on historic homes. The house made from two houses is the residence built in 1886 by John L. Darragh, president of the Galveston Wharf Company. As of this writing, it is for sale and in poor condition, as described, though the Galveston Historical Foundation is trying to save it. While I've taken a few literary liberties, the redbrick Italianate family home where Aunt Olivia and the others lived is modeled after Ashton Villa, built by John M. Brown, a prosperous businessman, in 1859. It has been restored and is open to the public. Tess's Moorish Gothic dream house was fashioned after the 1890 home of John Clement Trube. Until recently the dramatic old structure, sometimes called Trube Castle, existed as Tess and Dan saw it, but it is currently being restored for sale.

Jean Laffite was, of course, a real privateer who established Campeche on Galveston Island. There are many legends about his buried treasure, including stories about riches cached along an overland route through east Texas to St. Louis. The journal mentioned is in the Sam Houston Regional Library in Liberty, Texas, and is thought to be authentic. Laffite's friend, Aaron Cherry, owned property in the area where the cemetery was located. So far as I know, there was never any treasure buried there or at any of the other sites described, nor was Laffite married to the fictitious Contessa. While within the realm of historical *possibility*, the stories of Violet and her descendants, including Casey and Tess, and their connection to Laffite, were born entirely of my imagination.

THE EDITOR'S CORNER

We suspect that Cupid comes to visit our Bantam offices every year when we're preparing the Valentine's Day books. It seems we're always specially inspired by the one exclusively romantic holiday in the year. And our covers next month reflect just how inspired we were . . . by our authors who also must have had a visit from the chubby cherub. They shimmer with cherry-red metallic ink and are presents in and of themselves—as are the stories within. They range from naughty to very nice!

First, we bring you Suzanne Forster's marvelous **WILD CHILD**, LOVESWEPT #384. Cat D'Angelo had been the town's bad girl and Blake Wheeler its golden boy when the young assistant D.A. had sent her to the reformatory for suspected car theft. Now, ten years later, she has returned to work as a counselor to troubled kids—and to even the score with the man who had hurt her so deeply! Time had only strengthened the powerful forces that drew them together . . . and Blake felt inescapable hunger for the beautiful, complicated hellcat who could drive a man to ruin—or to ecstasy. Could the love and hate Cat had held so long in her heart be fused by the fire of mutual need and finally healed by passion? We think you'll find **WILD CHILD** delicious—yet calorie free—as chocolates packaged in a red satin box!

Treat yourself to a big bouquet with Gail Douglas's *The Dreamweavers:* **BEWITCHING LADY**, LOVESWEPT #385. When the Brawny Josh Campbell who looked as if he could wield a sword as powerfully as any clansman stopped on a deserted road to give her a ride, Heather Sinclair played a mischievous Scottish lass to the hilt, beguiling the moody but fascinating man whose gaze hid inner demons . . . and hinted at a dangerous passion she'd never known. Josh felt his depression lift after months of despair, but he was too cynical to succumb to this delectable minx's appeal . . . or was he? A true delight!

Sweet, fresh-baked goodies galore are yours in Joan
(continued)

Elliott Pickart's **MIXED SIGNALS,** LOVESWEPT #386. Katha Logan threw herself into Vince Santini's arms, determined to rescue the rugged ex-cop from the throng of reporters outside city hall. Vince enjoyed being kidnapped by this lovely and enchanting nut who drove like a madwoman and intrigued him with her story of a crime he just *had* to investigate . . . with her as his partner! Vince believed that a man who risked his life for a living had no business falling in love. Katha knew she could cherish Vince forever if he'd let her, but playing lovers' games wasn't enough anymore. Could they learn to fly with the angels and together let their passions soar?

We give a warm, warm greeting—covered with hearts, with flowers—to a new LOVESWEPT author, but one who's not new to any of us who treasure romances. Welcome Lori Copeland, who brings us LOVESWEPT #387, **DARLING DECEIVER,** next month. Bestselling mystery writer Shae Malone returned to the sleepy town where he'd spent much of his childhood to finish his new novel, but instead of peace and quiet, he found his home invaded by a menagerie of zoo animals temporarily living next door . . . with gorgeously grown-up Harriet Whitlock! As a teenager she'd chased him relentlessly, embarrassed him with poems declaring everlasting love, but now she was an exquisite woman whose long-legged body made him burn with white-hot fire. Harri still wanted Shae with shameless abandon, but did she dare risk giving her heart again?

Your temperature may rise when you read **HEART-THROB** by Doris Parmett, LOVESWEPT #388. Hannah Morgan was bright, eager, beautiful—an enigma who filled television director Zack Matthews with impatience . . . and a sizzling hunger. The reporter in him wanted to uncover her mysteries, while the man simply wanted to gaze at her in moonlight. Hannah was prepared to work as hard as she needed to satisfy the workaholic heartbreaker . . . until her impossibly virile boss crumbled her defenses with tenderness and ignited a hunger she'd never expected to feel again. Was she

(continued)

willing to fight to keep her man? Don't miss this sparkling jewel of a love story. A true Valentine's Day present.

For a great finish to a special month, don't miss Judy Gill's **STARGAZER,** LOVESWEPT #389, a romance that shines with the message of the power of love . . . at any age. As the helicopter hovered above her, Kathy M'Gonigle gazed with wonder at her heroic rescuer, but stormy-eyed Gabe Fowler was furious at how close she'd come to drowning in the sudden flood—and shocked at the joy he felt at touching her again! Years before, he'd made her burn with desire, but she'd been too young and he too restless to settle down. Now destiny had brought them both home. Could the man who put the stars in her eyes conquer the past and promise her forever?

All our books—well, their authors wish they could promise you forever. That's not possible, but authors and staff can wish you wonderful romance reading.

Now it is my great pleasure to give you one more Valentine's gift—namely, to reintroduce you to our Susann Brailey, now Senior Editor, who will grace these pages in the future with her fresh and enthusiastic words. But don't think for a minute that you're getting rid of me! I'll be here—along with the rest of the staff—doing the very best to bring you wonderful love stories all year long.

As I have told you many times in the past, I wish you peace, joy, and the best of all things—the love of family and friends.

Carolyn Nichols

Carolyn Nichols
Editor
LOVESWEPT
Bantam Books
666 Fifth Avenue
New York, NY 10103

FAN OF THE MONTH

Joni Clayton

It's really great fun to be a LOVESWEPT Fan of the Month as it provides me with the opportunity to publicly thank Carolyn Nichols, Bantam Books, and some of my favorite authors: Sandra Brown, Iris Johansen, Kay Hooper, Fayrene Preston, Helen Mittermeyer and Deborah Smith (to name only a few!).

My good friend, Mary, first introduced me to romance fiction and LOVESWEPTS in 1984 as an escape from the pressures of my job. Almost immediately my associates noticed the difference in my disposition and attitude and questioned the reason for the change. They all wanted to thank LOVESWEPT!

It did not take me long to discover that most romance series were inconsistent in quality and were not always to my liking—but not LOVESWEPT. I have thoroughly enjoyed each and every volume. All were "keepers" . . . so of course I wanted to own the entire series. I enlisted the aid of friends and used book dealers. Presto! The series was complete! As soon as LOVESWEPT was offered through the mail, I subscribed and have never missed a copy!

I have since retired from the "hurly-burly" of the working world and finally have the time to start to reread all of my LOVESWEPT "keepers."

To Carolyn, all of the authors, and the LOVESWEPT staff—Thanks for making my retirement so enjoyable!

60 Minutes to a Better, More Beautiful You!

Now it's easier than ever to awaken your sensuality, stay slim forever—even make yourself irresistible. With Bantam's bestselling subliminal audio tapes, you're only 60 minutes away from a better, more beautiful you!

__ 45004-2	**Slim Forever**	$8.95
__ 45112-X	**Awaken Your Sensuality**	$7.95
__ 45081-6	**You're Irresistible**	$7.95
__ 45035-2	**Stop Smoking Forever**	$8.95
__ 45130-8	**Develop Your Intuition**	$7.95
__ 45022-0	**Positively Change Your Life**	$8.95
__ 45154-5	**Get What You Want**	$7.95
__ 45041-7	**Stress Free Forever**	$7.95
__ 45106-5	**Get a Good Night's Sleep**	$7.95
__ 45094-8	**Improve Your Concentration**	$7.95
__ 45172-3	**Develop A Perfect Memory**	$8.95

Bantam Books, Dept. LT, 414 East Golf Road, Des Plaines, IL 60016

Please send me the items I have checked above. I am enclosing $_____ (please add $2.00 to cover postage and handling). Send check or money order, no cash or C.O.D.s please. (Tape offer good in USA only.)

Mr/Ms _____

Address _____

City/State _____ Zip _____

LT-12/89

Please allow four to six weeks for delivery.
Prices and availability subject to change without notice.

NEW!

Handsome Book Covers Specially Designed To Fit Loveswept Books

Our new French Calf Vinyl book covers come in a set of three great colors— royal blue, scarlet red and kachina green.

Each 7" × 9½" book cover has two deep vertical pockets, a handy sewn-in bookmark, and is soil and scratch resistant.

To order your set, use the form below.

THE DELANEY DYNASTY

Men and women whose loves an passions are so glorious it takes many great romance novels by three bestselling authors to tell their tempestuous stories.

THE SHAMROCK TRINITY

☐	21975	RAFE, THE MAVERICK *by Kay Hooper*	$2.95
☐	21976	YORK, THE RENEGADE *by Iris Johansen*	$2.95
☐	21977	BURKE, THE KINGPIN *by Fayrene Preston*	$2.95

THE DELANEYS OF KILLAROO

☐	21872	ADELAIDE, THE ENCHANTRESS *by Kay Hooper*	$2.75
☐	21873	MATILDA, THE ADVENTURESS *by Iris Johansen*	$2.75
☐	21874	SYDNEY, THE TEMPTRESS *by Fayrene Preston*	$2.75

THE DELANEYS: *The Untamed Years*

☐	21899	GOLDEN FLAMES *by Kay Hooper*	$3.50
☐	21898	WILD SILVER *by Iris Johansen*	$3.50
☐	21897	COPPER FIRE *by Fayrene Preston*	$3.50

Buy them at your local bookstore or use this page to order.

Bantam Books, Dept. SW7, 414 East Golf Road, Des Plaines, IL 60016

Please send me the items I have checked above. I am enclosing $_____ (please add $2.00 to cover postage and handling). Send check or money order, no cash or C.O.D.s please.

Mr/Ms _____

Address _____

City/State _____ Zip_____

SW7–11/89

Please allow four to six weeks for delivery.
Prices and availability subject to change without notice.